The news showed a clip of the new office tower growing out of control. Damn. What had gone wrong?

He checked messages and got Alison on the line.

"Alison, any news about what's caused the problem yet?"

"Jonathon said something went wrong with the tenting process. They've discovered the building just kept growing. It didn't cool down and die like it should have. Then it was cured prematurely, sealing in more heat. The damage has been done. They'll need to tear it down."

"Tear it down! Over my dead body." His father would approve of that.

"But there's something else. Jonathon wouldn't tell me, just that you need to call him."

"Okay, thanks."

"Good luck at the meeting," she said.

He snorted, amused and switched off the line. The damage had been done all right.

In the concrete parking garage of Futura Corp, the car pulled up next to the elevator and he got out.

Why did all these parking garages look the same? He could be anywhere in the world and it would be just another concrete bunker. Ugly and unimaginative.

He pulled his sleeve up and glanced at the phone. Five minutes before the meeting started.

"Jonathon Rodriguez," he spoke into the phone as he entered the elevator, filled with mirrors again, and punched in the floor number, then held his phone up for ID.

As the elevator moved upwards, a voice came over the phone, "Jonathon here,"

"Jonathon, it's Angus. Alison said you wanted to talk to me."

"Take me off speaker phone first."

"Okay, done," said Angus, holding his wrist up to his ear.

"So, she told you the building's still alive?"

"Yeah, but you killed it, right?"

"No. I can't. It's really alive. It's sentient," said Jonathon.

FALLING INTO FLIGHT

ALSO BY LINDA JORDAN:

Titanian Fury

Rescue Mission: Islands of Seattle, Book 1

To the Stars and Back Again

Notes on the Moon People

Faerie Unraveled: The Bones of the Earth Series, Book 1

The Black Opal: Jeweled Worlds Series, Book 1

Come on over to Linda's website and join the fun!

LindaJordan.net

Don't miss a new release!

Sign up for Linda's Serendipitous Newsletter while you're there.

FALLING INTO FLIGHT

LINDA JORDAN

For Michael & Zoe

CHAPTER 1 - ANGUS

IN HIS DREAM HER FACE HOVERED OVER HIM, PALE.

Why was he on his back? Had he fallen?

Angus could feel wind from her white wings, so large they pushed the fog around.

She wasn't an angel. He didn't believe in angels.

She was an air dancer.

And he was injured.

Angus rubbed his face, trying to wake up.

Finally his brain cooperated, came partially awake. He sat up, the sheets pooling around his waist in the dark room. He'd had the dream. Again.

Glancing at the clock, he read 6:40 a.m. Five minutes until the alarm went off. He groaned. Better face the damn day.

Angus moved his legs to the side of the large bed and flung off the soft sheets. He stood, walking to the sink in the corner of his bedroom. The lights came up slowly as he walked across the plushly carpeted room.

The scent of a cedar woodland was released in the air. Morning birdsong came over the sound system. All of it was supposed to be calming.

It wasn't.

He splashed cold water on his face, trying to wake up his body. His mind was already there.

He drank a glass of cold water to wash away the taste of sleep.

The mirror light switched on and the cabinet beside it slid open, the shelf with his razor extended out, offering it to him.

He quickly ran it over his face, cleaning off the last 24 hours of growth and noting the dark circles beneath his eyes.

His alarm clicked on with the morning news filling the screens in his bedroom.

"Off," he said. "I'm up."

The screens went blank and silence filled the room.

He couldn't face the news yet.

He pushed a button and the blinds opened. Light filtered through gray clouds entered the room. He looked out over the city.

It shimmered in half light of gray morning. Lights were on in all the buildings. Offices were starting up and apartments were being left behind. He lived in the business center of Queen Anne Island. New Seattle.

Parts of Old Seattle were still visible. The tops of old office towers that hadn't tumbled in the massive quake, flooded by the rising sea or been torn down by the scrappers. The scrappers lived out in the Bay, in the skeletons of the old buildings. Or floating on boats among them. Along with the homeless and the poor. The entire Bay was an ugly floating slum.

The other Islands of New Seattle glimmered in the morning. Capital Island, Beacon Island and off the the north, the mainland. Far off to the east sat Bellevue Island. Its offices towered even higher than New Seattle.

Angus ran his hands over his face. He dreaded the meeting this morning. With his father and the other directors. He'd need to do heavy damage control.

He preferred to stay in the dream. Find out who she was. She of the delicate features with dove gray eyes and white spiky hair. She who had long arms and legs. And wings of the softest feathers. And a tall, slender body.

He shook himself back to reality. He couldn't be late.

Did it matter? They were going to hang him out to twist in the wind of bad publicity anyway.

There would be time to wonder about her later.

He added a touch of tint to his face, which covered up most of the darkness beneath his eyes. Then ran a brush through his curly dark hair and stood in the dry shower for a few minutes until it cycled off.

Her face hovered in his consciousness as he dressed in the unofficial uniform of Futura Corp. Black shoes, white shirt, blue suit and that damn tie. It was the twenty second century and Earth was still living in the past.

Angus ate a cinnamon spice breakfast bar with his bitter coffee as he rode the mirrored elevator down to the parking garage to pick up his car. He got into the sleek looking black vehicle and punched in the default destination. Then settled in to watch the morning's news while the car drove. It was raining out now, covering the windows with water.

What else was new? It was Seattle after all. Everything here was gray and dreary. Gray buildings, gray sky, gray lives.

The news showed a clip of the new office tower growing out of control. Damn. What had gone wrong?

He checked messages and got Alison on the line.

"Alison, any news about what's caused the problem yet?"

"Jonathon said something went wrong with the tenting process. They've discovered the building just kept growing. It didn't cool down and die like it should have. Then it was cured prematurely, sealing in more heat. The damage has been done. They'll need to tear it down."

"Tear it down! Over my dead body." His father would approve of that.

3

"But there's something else. Jonathon wouldn't tell me, just that you need to call him."

"Okay, thanks."

"Good luck at the meeting," she said.

He snorted, amused and switched off the line. The damage had been done all right.

In the concrete parking garage of Futura Corp, the car pulled up next to the elevator and he got out.

Why did all these parking garages look the same? He could be anywhere in the world and it would be just another concrete bunker. Ugly and unimaginative.

He pulled his sleeve up and glanced at the phone. Five minutes before the meeting started.

"Jonathon Rodriguez," he spoke into the phone as he entered the elevator, filled with mirrors again, and punched in the floor number, then held his phone up for ID.

As the elevator moved upwards, a voice came over the phone, "Jonathon here,"

"Jonathon, it's Angus. Alison said you wanted to talk to me."

"Take me off speaker phone first."

"Okay, done," said Angus, holding his wrist up to his ear.

"So, she told you the building's still alive?"

"Yeah, but you killed it, right?"

"No. I can't. It's really alive. It's sentient," said Jonathon.

"What?"

"It's sentient. It's not just some dumb plant, like the ones that line your office windows."

"How is that possible?" asked Angus, his chest tightening.

"I don't know."

"How do you know it's sentient?"

"The growth that's happening, it's not just random. It's creating a building like we've never seen. And it's doing it with intelligence. I don't know how to explain it, but you've got to come to the site."

4

"That's it?" asked Angus. "That it's got a plan?"

"It's also learning. If that's not intelligence, I don't know what is."

Angus sighed, exasperated.

"I'll try to make it after the meeting."

"I wouldn't mention this at the meeting."

"Why?"

"I think you should come look first. I don't think we want to get boardroom politics involved in this. Not yet. This is important. I can't put enough emphasis on that. This has never happened before. Ever. It could be the breakthrough we've been searching for?"

"Seriously, you think an out of control building is a good thing?" asked Angus, as the elevator stopped and the doors opened.

He walked out into the corridor, towards the meeting room.

"Just come to the site. I'll be here. No chance I'm leaving. Too much going on here."

"Okay, well I'm here. I'll talk to you later," said Angus.

The others were already there, getting coffee and pastries, finding their seats. He was late, having missed the pre-meeting socializing. Something he'd always prided himself on. Keeping up on people's lives. Mingling was important for management.

The silence that descended on the room told him they'd been talking about him. He tried to ignore the discomfort, but this morning it wasn't coming easily.

Angus nodded and said, "Good morning."

"Good morning," echoed several voices.

Then he picked up a mug, poured coffee from the dispenser and put a scone on a plate. He grabbed a napkin and took his seat.

The scone was blueberry and the buttery pastry nearly melted in his mouth.

Angus ignored the chitchat about the previous weekend and

weighed his options. Should he keep quiet about this newest development? Or speak up, using it as a promise of things to come?

Jonathon had a distrust of all politics and his advice needed to be tempered with that in mind. But he'd stressed the importance of silence about what was happening. And Angus didn't really know what was happening, so he couldn't extrapolate on the possibilities.

Well, he'd just have to wing it and see what needed to be said today.

His father and Jenna, his father's assistant, came in. His father wore the same suit as everyone else, but with a gold lapel pin. A pin he'd gotten from his father as a thank you for serving the company. One Angus wasn't likely to inherit.

Everyone was there now.

Twelve people Angus needed to convince this wasn't a total disaster.

CHAPTER 2 - CAER

CAER STOOD AT THE BARRE, STRETCHING HER LONG LEGS. THE massive, airy room with a three story ceiling felt cold this morning, even through her drab colored warm up clothes, layers of leotards, tights, wraps and ballet shoes. Her hair pulled tight into a bun.

The room was empty. No one else was there yet. She liked being first. It made her feel powerful and more dedicated than anyone else. Better than the others.

Dawn spilled in through the huge wall of windows that she could see out of, but no one could see in. The company demanded privacy in their rehearsal space.

She could feel the tension in her calves and breathed into the knots, trying to release them. Willing her body to let go of the world and give itself over to the music running through her mind. To let go of the Earth and do what it had been born to do.

She extended each huge wing, stretching it to the extreme, feeling the muscles tighten and then relax.

Unlike the other members of the troupe, she'd been born with wings and thinned, elongated bones. She'd still had the painful injections to strengthen her bones, but her wings had come out of the womb with her. The others' wings were grafted on. And their bones lengthened and thinned by many hours under the knife and all the drugs they'd been required to take, which had awful side affects.

She heard scuffling behind her and gazed into the mirrored wall in front of her.

Margaux was here. She was the head of the company, which meant this was an important rehearsal. She wore royal blue to match the blue feathers in her wings. And her hair was permanently dyed blue. During performances she used to dye her skin blue as well.

Sonya was the choreographer for this piece. Margaux wasn't normally here.

Caer continued to stretch out as the other dancers filed in. No one spoke, they concentrated on their own bodies.

All except Margaux, who watched everything. She made Caer nervous. Caer knew the woman missed nothing.

She was still an extraordinary dancer, one of the first generation of fliers, but her grafts failed several years ago. She couldn't fly like she used to. Her wings were little more than cosmetic now.

Margaux had been unable to qualify for new ones. The government sold the program to the Bacchus Corp. Now they had stricter qualifications to get in and the process cost a fortune. Margaux was too old to qualify.

Soon, the dancers wouldn't need the whole process any more. Caer was just the first of the babies born with wings. There were already six more, the oldest was five years behind her. But there would be more. Their little company would grow organically now, not surgically.

Hands clapped. She turned to see Sonya in the middle of the floor.

Sonya wore red, as usual. To match her red wings and permanently dyed hair.

"Attention Dancers. Before we start, I'd like to make a change for today. We will *not* be using trails today. But we'll do the full ballet but without props. After Margaux makes an announcement." She gracefully moved her arm as a gesture to invite Margaux to speak.

Margaux moved to the center of the room, every movement poetry. Caer could have watched the woman do anything. She certainly wasn't slowed down by her pain.

"Hello everyone," said Margaux, in a deep smoky voice.

The room was absolutely silent, Margaux held everyone's complete attention.

"I'm sorry to interrupt your rehearsal time, but I thought you'd want to know. We've had a request to add an additional performance to our schedule. A one off for the Spears Corporation. They're our most reliable donor and cover forty percent of our operating costs, so we're talking about a huge chunk of money. It's part of their stockholder's meeting. If we accept their request, it will mean a week with no rest day. It will be a full performance and in one of their buildings. They have security concerns, of course. But that means extra rehearsal time for us to cram into our busy schedule. I don't see how we can say no and expect them to continue their financial support. But, I wanted to ask all of you if we could make it work? You're the ones who will be most impacted." She cocked her head as if asking for comments.

"Can we cancel another performance?" asked Tanyth.

"No, all sold out," said Margaux.

"We'll need more backups," said Colin. "We'll have injuries."

"We can pull from the classes. Have those who are qualified be understudies. So we have extras," said Margaux.

"I don't see that we have any choice," said John. He was the oldest dancer still performing. He was also Caer's father, although they weren't close, he was very protective of her. "We've struggled for years to get funded. It's been a hard road. We can't let it slip out of our grip now."

Margaux nodded her head in agreement.

"Does anyone object to doing this?" asked Margaux.

No one raised their hand.

"Okay then, I'll begin drawing up an understudy schedule. Some of you may have to add in an additional part to learn. I'll try to get it posted by the end of the day."

Margaux nodded to Sonya that she was finished and left the center of the room. She took the quick lift to the top level to watch the rehearsal.

The quick lift was little more than an open metal platform with a handhold which operated on an electronic pulley system. It worked silently, normally used by dancers to take them, unseen, to their starting places on different levels of the building.

"Okay everyone, get to your places. We're starting at the top of Act II."

Caer stripped her leggings and extra sweater off, tossing them in a corner. She flew to the top western corner of the room and grabbed a hook in the ceiling, her feet on the wall, bracing herself, waiting for the music to begin. Excitement pulsed through her. She loved this part of the ballet.

She hung there, excitement building in her. She breathed deeply, forcing herself to relax and focus.

The music started up slowly. This was a new ballet, created last year, and the music seemed to be a collision between Debussy, new age swirliness and retro-metal. It was filled with drama almost to the point of passing as opera, but without the singing.

Perfect for Air Dancing.

Jeanie began her descent, a slow dive into the room, spinning until she reached center. Then she leveled off as the violins increased and hovered in one place, flapping and as she began to act out the despair in her heart at the loss of her family. The war had taken them from her.

Then came the drums and the gray men, all ten of them flew to the center of the room, circling in a precise, military style. They would look identical in their costumes. Now only one of them was gray, the others would have to dye themselves for the weeks of performances. Their short, muscular wings were perfect for this type of movement. They didn't get tangled up with each other.

Jeanie fluttered to the side of the room, attaching herself to a corner, hiding, her wings curling around herself, her back to the center.

John flew into the middle of the gray men. He would be black. The commander, he gave orders for them to move out. Their circle widened to the edges of the room, where their wings would create a wind moving across the audiences' faces on that level, before the gray men flew offstage.

John remained behind, hiding in another corner, watching for just a few moments, then flew out himself.

Jeanie flew to the center again and was comforted by several other women, all of them having lost people in the war.

Caer would be in white. She twirled through the air, joined by Trina, dressed all in black. They swirled around each other far above the other women, long wingtips brushing. That closeness always sent a rush of fear through Caer. A broken wing and she'd fall and break too. Then they joined, Trina wrapping her arms around Caer's waist, their wings beating in tandem.

Caer and Trina flew from the heights as the music rose again. Their wings expanded to full width and they seemingly floating down from the heavens. The avenging angels. They comforted Jeanie and promised revenge for her losses and for the other women as well.

The other women left and Caer and Trina stayed with Jeanie, showing her how to flirt. Down below them flew a lone gray man.

This one younger and more heroic than the others. A darker gray, but not yet black like the commander. Colin was alone. Spinning in circles, practicing maneuvers and contemplating.

They sent Jeanie, all in blush pink, to run into him, accidentally, while they hovered in a corner.

Jeanie and Colin met. She flirted, he fell in love with her. She led him on, or did she?

Was she falling in love as well? They made plans to meet later that night and exited.

Then Caer and Trina danced, moving around the entire performance space, claiming it, diving in and out around each other. Caer had to move fast to keep up with Trina's quick movements. Her shorter wings made her more agile. Caer balanced that with her superior strength and grace. Caer moved as if deciding the bargain wouldn't work, Trina chasing her, wanting her power. They ended up entwined again and left the stage.

Off stage Caer stood on the third level, panting. Catching her breath. This role was the most challenging thing she'd done yet. She'd only been a full member of the company for two years. And most of her time onstage had been an ensemble member, not a principal dancer. Her wings just hadn't been strong enough, she'd been too young. And she hadn't fit in as an ensemble member. Her wings were too long, ostentatious and fluffy. But now they were stronger, at least.

Trina was panting too, although she regained her breath control faster. Her short wings had always fit into the ensemble and she'd gotten onstage more often. She was a year or two ahead of Caer, even though she'd never be as showy.

Their next entrance was on Level 5. Caer followed Trina up the back stairs, leaving the quick lift for those who had less time between exits and entrances. They perched on the edge of the stage watching the other dancers below.

A battle roared on Levels 1 and 3. Thirty gray and red dancers fought with blunted swords. Caer marveled at the dancers' agility. They had to execute the choreography perfectly to avoid getting hit my a sword. Looking down from this level was the best. The patterns the dancers wove was extraordinary. She could feel the pain and anguish. During the performance they would have packets of fake blood beneath their costumes that could be punctured. Which would of course drip down on dancers below, but also spray on the audience from the wind caused by wings. Audiences were given damp towels and were warned not to dress up for this ballet. Emphasizing the ugliness of war was part of the point.

In the center on Level 2, Gregor and John, the two commanders were locked in a struggle. They were swordless and wrestling.

Holding onto each other, scarlet and black, perfectly balanced and pushing out from the other, wings pounding the air. The other dancers stayed a level away. Their pummeling wings creating a wind that Gregor and John would have had to fight against. The two battled for what seemed like an eternity, until John finally choked Gregor into unconsciousness. He let himself fall. Caught by the reds fighting below.

The black and grays did a victory lap around the upper levels and exited. The reds carried their downed leader around the blood stained lower levels and mourned.

Act I ended.

Caer leaned back and let out her breath. The actual performance couldn't get much better than this. It would have costumes and lighting and the dancers would use emissions, colored vapor trails, but the basic performance was thrilling. There would also be effect-aroma working along with the ballet. She felt honored to be a part of this company.

Trina stood and said, "C'mon, time to stretch out."

Caer stood and in the cramped space stretched her wings.

There would be a 15 minute intermission during the performance, but not now.

They'd just finished stretching when the Act II music started up. Caer wrapped her arms around Trina's waist and they dove. Now it was her turn to have complete trust. Darkness was in charge now. All she could do was follow.

CHAPTER 3 - ANGUS

ANGUS SAT IN THE BACK OF HIS CAR, WATCHING THE GRAYNESS OF Seattle move past the rain streaked windows.

The meeting had gone about as badly as he'd expected. This whole project was a train wreck. He'd been given a two week deadline to turn the PR mess around and a month to get his company back on track. The Board hadn't known what to do about the building, but basically, he had to turn this into a shining achievement. Somehow. In a month.

He rubbed his face, wishing he could turn into someone else. He grabbed his coffee from the cup holder and drank some of the bitter lukewarm liquid.. It was his fourth cup today and his stomach roiled in rebellion. He should get some lunch. But he didn't tell the car to stop.

As the car pulled up to the construction site he saw that the building had grown even more than the shots from the morning news. It had grown an arm sideways. Forming a walkway between it and the building next door, also a 'grown' building, but unfinished inside and not occupied yet. That one was already dead, though.

The whole thing didn't look good. If it infected the unfinished building next to it, they could lose both of them. That would kill the company.

Angus got out and hurried through the driving rain until he was under the canopy set up as a workstation.

Jonathon Rodriquez was there with part of his team. His face looked grim, constricted and pinched. The man hadn't slept, he was wearing clothes that were at least a day old, maybe two.

"Angus, glad you could come," he said, gripping Angus' hand with both of his.

"So, what's going on?"

"Come on inside," said Jonathon.

"Is it safe?"

"Hell, I don't know," Jonathon said. "It's sentient. I really don't know what it'll do next. None of the other buildings have seen us as a threat. I'd be careful about keeping your intentions quiet and buried deep inside. Just be open to seeing what this building has to add to the city."

What the hell did that mean? That he shouldn't talk about killing it? All their 'grown' buildings got killed. Otherwise, they wouldn't stop growing. And it had been hell to get permits for them as it was. New Seattle was wary of innovation after its past. The building's death was written into those permits and contracts. It was part of the construction process.

Angus followed Jonathon inside the pinkish gray structure. The dye was normally added just before the building was killed. The building was planned to be a warm sky blue color. The walls pulsed with fluid, sending information and instructions to the building. Telling it how deep to grow its roots and many floors tall to become. How wide. How many rooms on each floor. How to grow elevator shafts and make stairwells and windows in each room. The 'skin' was warm and soft to the touch, unlike the hardened 'skin' of dead buildings.

He touched it, feeling the life throbbing inside.

It smelled clean somehow. Not the soapy clean of new sheets, but a clean like fresh clean air off the ocean. Unpolluted air. Which was hard to find these days. But the growing buildings would help that. Each building that grew cleaned the air as long as it was alive. If every city was growing a building or two, what a different place the world would be.

The warmth of its skin filled the empty space of the building. They climbed up flight after flight of stairs. Then they got to the walkway. The structure inside looked completely different.

Instead of the round empty tube that buildings normally were programmed to grow, before floors were filled in, this was a hexagon. Sharp, sleek edges and hard 'skin'. Windows filled the top three sides, enclosed by strong supports. The tube, about forty feet wide, had opened up the other building.

Jonathon started across the walkway and when Angus hesitated, he said, "Come on. It's as safe as anywhere."

Inside the other building, the first one had begun growing a new skin inside the dead one. As if repairing the dead building.

"We think it's attempting to resurrect this building. Grow a completely new skin over the dead one and ..."

"Why?"

"Because it's a growing machine. That's what we've programmed it to be. To heal any damage caused during construction."

"But why did it override the template we gave it? Why did it add the walkway? Why has it grown taller and wider than we asked?"

"I don't know. There must have been a mistake somewhere. We've looked and looked. Checked the original programming. Checked the initial growth cells, making sure they're not contaminated by anything. We haven't an answer for that yet."

"Well, I don't need to tell you that the Board's livid. I've got two weeks to transform this PR disaster, and that's generous on their part. And another month to deal with the actual building. To make everything work. So building, don't know exactly how conscious you are, but we need some help here. I want to be able to keep growing buildings like you. Help us out here."

Angus didn't really expect an answer. Of any kind. This was for Jonathon's benefit. He needed to know that there was a firm termination date for this project.

Jonathon snorted and said, "It's all about intent and energy. The building reads that. Not actual words."

"Energy? All I got is panic. Sheer panic," said Angus.

"Well, that's not helpful. But I'd like to think that this building is smarter than we are. If you go further in, which is difficult right now, the building is exploring the other building's electrical, plumbing and air circulation systems that we've added. And it's modifying them. We're not quite sure how yet, engineers are still studying the changes. But they've said, they don't understand exactly how the building is making changes, but they've been energy saving and more environmentally stable. It's like the building is taking our technology and streamlining it. Making it better and more functional. At least that's their theory. The lead electrical engineer said she's learning a huge amount. 'The building is being wired in completely unconventional ways, which are stunningly more effective.' Her words," said Jonathon.

"So, you think we should just let the building keep growing."

"Yeah, we're having major breakthroughs here. It would be a shame to lose this. And, yes it puts not one, but two buildings behind schedule, but I think our gains will inevitably outweigh the lost time."

Angus stared at him. Perhaps he could spin this for the media. For the company.

"Okay, I've seen enough. I've got to get back. Can you write up something for me? A list of benefits for keeping this project going? Get it to me by the end of today?"

Jonathon raised an eyebrow at him. "Isn't that your job?"

"Yeah, but I want it with all the scientific jargon. And with your opinion. You see things that I don't. It's my job to spin it so the media and the Directors can understand. To sell it."

"Yeah, yeah, yeah. I'll get something to you today," said Jonathon.

They went back down the stairs and Angus called his car.

He tried not to breathe deeply. Not take in the pollen filled air outside. Every year, every decade it had gotten worse, since global warming began. This was a day he should have stayed inside completely, like most people did.

As he got into the car, he noticed the yellow dust covering it, despite the rain. Pollen. He'd go home, toss his clothes in the laundry and shower. A wet one this time. Then set to work on figuring out how to dig out of this disaster.

And see if he could find that woman. The one who'd been showing up in his dreams every night for a year now.

CHAPTER 4 - CAER

CAER RODE THE CRAMPED, BEAT UP, METAL ELEVATOR DOWN TO THE basement theater and meeting room with John. They were very noticeably not talking.

The smell of sweaty bodies filled the air. It had already taken several loads of dancers down. She sipped from her water bottle, but the water was warm and a day or two old. It tasted stale. She needed to wash the steel bottle and fill it with fresh water tomorrow.

Her muscles felt cramped. She wanted to stretch, but then she'd have to acknowledge that she wanted to take up more than her share of space in the elevator.

She'd have to acknowledge him.

He was pissed off at her and she was just as angry at him. She was eighteen now. Officially of age. And he was still trying to push her around like she was an eight year old girl. She hadn't been eight since he'd left her and Mom. He had no right to tell her who she could date.

And it had been just a date. A simple lunch date on their one day off. She and Elias, one of the dancers, who was in the red army for this show, had gone out to eat. At that trendy new melange restaurant on the Mainland. The meal had taken hours. And the media had seen them. It was a big deal, lots of photos on the news.

John had a screaming fit. In the rehearsal room, after the final rehearsal. In front of everyone.

Caer stood up for herself. Elias had said it was probably good publicity. She tended to agree, but wouldn't have said it. But she felt too embarrassed and enraged at having her personal life outed in the rehearsal room.

Then John accused her of not being able to control her emotions. Of being too susceptible to the effect-aroma used by the Special Effects Techs.

She shut down then and refused to say anything. That was preposterous. Insulting. And possibly true. But she'd never admit to it. Nor would any dancer. They trained their minds every day to be able to withstand the pheromones and other chemicals used to induce mood changes in the audiences.

A dancer had to be able to focus on the dance, not on the anger or agony raging through the air. If a dancer couldn't do that, they risked injury to everyone onstage, including themselves. It was one of the first lessons they learned. To control their emotions. To take care of yourself, so you wouldn't hurt anyone else. Everyone was connected.

Marie, the Costumer, had pulled John off to get a fitting.

Everyone else was horrified. Some were so embarrassed they said nothing and left. Others took her side and apologized for John. But she knew that no one would ever look at her the same again. They'd be looking for signs that she didn't have the control needed.

Every. Time. She. Took. To. The. Air.

So, two days later, here they were. Silence hung in the air, making the elevator ride smothering. She felt almost claustrophobic.

Caer's anger had grown every day. And no apology was forthcoming. But she would not break. Her anger was under control and would stay that way.

So were the feelings of hurt and rejection.

The door opened and she got out first. The hallway was filled with dancers and staff, moving into the large theatre. The last rehearsal had been recorded. They'd all watch it and get final notes before opening night. Tomorrow.

She sat on the carpeted floor of the theatre, her wings bent up at the tips. She made a half-hearted attempt to stretch out. Worn out more from the psychological strain of holding in the anger and hurt and trying to be perfect, than from the actual dress rehearsal.

The room filled.

Sonja went to the front of the room and waited until everyone was silent.

"Okay, after the showing, we'll have notes. I'll do dancers first, so you can go rest before tomorrow's opening, and then we'll do tech notes. Let's go," she said, her forearm making a whirling motion.

Sonja went to sit on a stool, her wings draping down the back. She pulled out a small pad to type notes on.

The movie of the rehearsal was well shot. The camera had stayed in one section, high up, maybe Level 4, and caught almost all the action.

Caer saw a couple of places where she could have done better. Made cleaner transitions between movements. And there was a particularly clumsy moment between her and Trina; they needed to do something different there. She glanced at Trina who was looking at her and stuck her finger in her mouth, making a gagging motion. Caer nodded in agreement.

The film took as long as the rehearsal. She glanced at her phone and groaned inwardly. Not much rest or sleep tonight. It was 1:23 a.m.

Then the notes strung out forever and were almost all about the two armies and battles. The battle choreography was incredibly complicated.

Caer tried to be patient and not squirm. She concentrated on giving herself feet and calf massages, while listening.

Sonya hadn't caught the clumsy action with her and Trina and Caer had no notes at all, actually. So fuck you John. I do fine with the effect-aroma.

When the dancers were excused at 3:10 a.m., she caught Trina and they practiced the move in the hallway a couple of times, until they found a smoother transition. Then took an empty elevator up to the bridge level and went to their separate apartments.

Caer's apartment consisted of a bedroom, bathroom and a third room which held a vintage chaise lounge, an antique metal and formica kitchen table with old wooden stools and a tiny kitchen in the corner. It was small by dancers' standards, but it was all hers and she loved it.

Air dancers needed larger spaces because of their wings. The larger the wings, the more space they took up. Furniture, clothing and bedding were all different than for the non-winged.

She tossed her dirty clothes on the bedroom floor and slid into her bed, lying face down. The heat was high enough, she didn't need any blanket except her large wings.

Then she was suddenly wide awake. She knew there would be no sleep until she cried out her hurt and tension. She dwelled on John's accusation, trying to get it all out.

Why did John hate her? Why had he accused her of being weak? Was he trying to get her dumped from the company? Was he trying to ruin her life? He'd never been a Dad to her, ever, so why was he trying now? Or was he?

Then she cried about how lonely she felt. She'd never had a lover, never had time. Her only friends were other dancers and they were too busy, as was she, to be close to anyone.

Still she longed for a lover, someone she could love deeply and passionately. And someone who would love her in return. No matter how badly or brilliantly she danced.

Finally exhausted, she fell into troubled sleep.

CHAPTER 5 - ANGUS

THAT EVENING ANGUS PACED HIS ROOMS. HE'D TURNED THE DECOR to green, which was supposed to be relaxing. It wasn't working.

He felt exhausted and keyed up all at the same time.

Soft, ethereal music played over the sound system. Soaring fiddles playing Celtic music combined with chimes from somewhere else and Indian tabla drums. A woman's voice sang in Hindi. The effect was enchanting. He longed to get lost in the music.

He'd put cedar forest in the scent selector and it permeated the room, obliterating the smell of the leftover curried chicken he'd had for dinner. He sipped mint water, hoping to make it up to his stomach. He'd had far too much coffee today.

Angus talked to the screens, then deleted things he'd said, until he had something to run by the PR department. It wasn't good enough, though. He'd need to come up with more information than Jonathon's team had given him.

He ran his hand through his unkempt hair. No matter how he tried, he couldn't stop thinking about her. And the dream. It had gone farther this morning.

She touched him. Brushed his face with her fingers.

He could still feel the sensation, even though he'd been awake all day.

He had to find her. Find out who she was. She had wings, which made it probable she was an air dancer or a government employee. When she first started appearing in his dreams, when he first noticed her wings, he'd done some research.

The first 'flyers' were made about twenty five years ago. In response to a string of natural disasters. Lack of resources, oil and gas, kickstarted many programs, including the genetically modified human ones. Amphibious humans, flying humans, people who could see in the dark, so many modifications were tried. Some were spectacular and those programs kept going. Others were failures and abandoned. Making people who could fly was a long and painful process and few opted for it. Mechanical eyes in the sky became more feasible as new technologies were discovered.

Flying humans left for the arts. Most for the new art form which had sprung up called air dancing. It merged ballet, modern dance and flying. And apparently it was breathtaking. He'd never seen it.

He had no name for her and had searched the three largest national air dancing companies. Photos of the dancers were available, but she wasn't there. She might be too young though. It took years of training to become a principal dancer. And years of injections, bone thinning and strengthening grafts, and other unpleasantness. Which was why the federal program had died. People didn't want to go through that much pain for a government job. But for art, people were always willing to go through amazing amounts of suffering. It had always been that way.

Angus had decided to hire an artist to create a drawing of her, and then a private detective. He didn't have the time and resources to search on his own. But he couldn't stop thinking about her. And a year's worth of dreams wasn't just a whim. She was someone he needed to know or she wouldn't be showing up in his dreams every night.

She was his soul mate.

He'd never had time for a partner and had only dated casually. Women tried to seduce him more often than he liked. They thought he was screaming rich.

It wasn't well known that his father had denied him an inheritance, other than running the company of his choice from amongst the Corporation's holdings. He'd done the same for Angus' older brother, Jonas. Jonas had chosen a safe bet for his company and made a success of it.

So, two years ago Angus had chosen Core Growth Industries, an exotic and risky choice, but he believed passionately that it was important for the world to take those risks.

He had to make it work or he was out of a job. And really any other options. If he failed, he'd have to find a job and work, just like everyone else on the planet.

And his company wasn't looking too good at the moment. Their two biggest building projects were mating and growing out of control. Every hour since the first newscasts, his company was worth less. Investors pulling out.

Tomorrow morning he had an interview on the Strobus Report. The top rated business show on right now. He'd have to do some fancy talking to keep up.

He pulled up the current stock rating. It had dropped again. He sent a message to his broker to buy more shares. At least the stock was affordable now. He sent a message to Jonathon and his team, and all the other company employees, pointing out that if they believed in the company, now was a good time to buy. Before he made announcements tomorrow on the show.

He sat and wrote a carefully worded report to the Board, about what he'd found out today. Pointing out that the two buildings had become a hotbed of ground breaking research, which would be salable, and a bonus to the two innovative buildings.

That Core Growth Industries was pointing the way into the future. Their new catchphrase was 'We got there first'. Or something like that. He needed advertising to work on it and sent them a message. He needed something by 10 a.m.

There was nothing else he could do tonight. Tomorrow he needed to look rested and relaxed. Confidant. He needed to sleep.

And dream of her.

CHAPTER 6 - CAER

CAER CROUCHED IN THE WINGS OF FLOOR 5, WATCHING THE SCENE below. The audience was filling up the seats, chattering amongst themselves. This space felt strange to her. The Speares Corporation Building was huge. The performance space the dancers were using was ten feet wider and longer than what the Company normally used. The height of the core was three feet shorter. The net was two feet closer to the floor to make up for it. She hoped no one needed it tonight. Of course she hoped that every night. A lack of dancers falling from the air was a good thing.

She licked her lips, tasting the oily, thin white makeup which coated her skin, making it even more pale. She'd temporarily made her hair white to match her wings.

The walls were painted a dull gray, making them a little difficult to see under the lights. And the lights were in strange places, this office building didn't have all the rigging that their own performance space did, so lights had been attached differently to illuminate the space adequately.

It smelled like an office building, scented with their own mix of effect-aroma to encourage industriousness, she guessed. She couldn't place any of the scents though. It wasn't unpleasant, just dull. Well, that would change.

Twenty minutes before the show started, the company's masters would get to work and fill the place with conflict and aggression and love.

They were six performances into the run of this ballet and most of the problems had been shaken out. They'd had two rehearsals in this office space, on Saturday and Sunday mornings when the offices were closed, with normal performances each of those nights. And here they were on Monday, normally a day off, performing again.

Everyone was feeling the exhaustion. It might save the Company, financially, but it was on the back of the dancers and techs. The exhaustion would really come when next weekend rolled around and performances and rehearsals were on their gazillionth day straight.

Caer heard the elevator swish open behind the tunnel and people came out of it.

The techs had the seemingly impossible task of turning the dinging off in those elevators, so whenever a dancer took one up to Floor 5, the bloody elevator wouldn't make noise, interrupting the performance.

And the airflow problems. Sheesh. The building had air currents that swept through its open central corridor that were akin to wind. It was awful.

The techs finally got it sorted so that the circulation system could be turned off for several hours at a time. It was hard enough to fly up five floors when you were exhausted, but even worse when you were flying against the wind.

Their wings created enough wind.

The audience members for this floor were filing in now. They were dressed down, wearing baggy pants and shirts. Washable stuff. They'd been warned about flying liquids. The lower floors would be the management of the Spear Corporation's various companies.

This floor was where the directors of the corporation would sit. Along with their families. They wore much more elegant clothes, even for dressing down.

Caer didn't even wear clothes this fancy when she went out on her day off.

One man, sitting close to the tunnel where she crouched, caught her eye. Really handsome, in a classical movie actor sort of way. Dark, slightly curled hair, blue eyes, cheekbones that stood out.

He was busily typing messages into a phone, his eyebrows wrinkled together in worry. He wore a suit, as if he hadn't had time to change. It looked rumpled, as if he'd been wearing it more than a day.

Another man sat down beside him and they began to talk. The other man looked quite a bit like the first, older, maybe they were brothers. He was dressed in olive green workout clothes.

She put her ear to the side of the fabric tunnel, straining to hear their conversation.

The older one said, "I assume you've seen the headlines or a newscast?"

"No," said the younger one, stopping typing.

"I hate to tell you, the press didn't go for your story. They saw the spin on it, I'm afraid."

"It wasn't spin. It was the truth. Damn."

"I know. I liked the idea of growing buildings. Tough luck, little brother," said the older one, then he turned to his female companion and began talking.

The other man went back to his typing. He looked like his life depended on it.

Caer's legs needed to move, so she retreated back out of the tunnel and went into a meeting room that had been designated for the dancers' use. She stretched her calves again, fluttering her wings to keep them warmed up.

The com came on, "Places everyone, break a wing."

She left the room, closing the door and was on her way to the tunnel, when she almost ran into the typing man. He wasn't watching where he was going.

"Oh, excuse me," he said, glancing up, then he stared at her in surprise.

"Leaving so soon, the performance hasn't even started," she said.

"Um, just taking a break. I've got a lot going on. I'll be back," he said, smiling at her. "I'll certainly be back.

She nodded and went into the tunnel, crouching as she moved towards the mouth. The audience lights were going down and the stage lights coming up. She could smell the deep scent of fear, wafting its way out of the atomizers. She breathed deep, feeling calmness fill her body. Focus on the performance, focus on your body, focus on the dance. The music began thrumming. She could see Kira perched in her tube on Floor 3, ready to fly.

There it was, the passage just before her action. On the exact note, she plunged down the central tube of the building, spinning in a circle, the others weaving around her.

She was the most visible, being all white. The other dancers were all colored and the pattern worked better that way. She pulled up, just before the net and began ascending, her wings working hard on the tight turns.

Ginny was out of place. Caer felt their wingtips brush. Ginny moved farther off. Back into position. The whole first section felt slightly off. No one was used to the dimensions of this space. As they moved through the dance, things got better though.

But not perfect.

The sharp peppery scent of conflict and anger filled the

space. Along with staccato violins. The first dancers flew offstage as the red army appeared. Caer was the last to leave, hovering above them in a red light. A foreshadowing of things to come. Then she flew off into the tunnel on Floor 4.

She crawled through the tunnel, her big wings brushing the top and went into the dancers' room. Following Mari and Kira. Inside the room with the door closed, she blotted her face on a towel and checked her white makeup. It was still holding. They each stood in front of fans, drying their feathers. Trying to cool off. Catch their breath.

She had fifteen minutes to get back to the fifth level for her first interlude with Trina. The beginning of the battle between good and evil.

Caer stretched and then left the room, walking to the elevator. She waited several minutes for the elevator.

It didn't come.

She didn't have time to stand around here.

What the hell was holding up the elevator?

She ran for the stairwell and then up two flights, cursing all the way. She got to the fifth floor and stood panting and trying to catch her breath. She peered into the dancer's room at the monitor.

About two minutes till she was on again.

Caer tried to calm herself and catch her breath as she crawled back down the tunnel. Crouching and waiting for her cue. Typing man wasn't there.

Focus.

Focus on the dance.

Her eyes blurred with tears. The atomizers were in hyperdrive. Her eyes burned with chili peppers. She hoped they got it sorted out soon. She could barely see.

Wiping her eyes, she heard her cue and floated down over the battle scene below. All the dancers, who were supposed to be alive, were carrying off 'dead' dancers. She saw their eyes streaming with tears.

Hopefully, they'd tell someone and get it fixed.

The air was wafting out to the audience members and some of them were in tears.

The sad, grief filled music rolled over the end of the battle music as she surveyed the battle scene. Colin, a dark gray, hovered, held his wounded arm while he watched his soldiers carry off their dead. He fluttered over the battlefield vowing revenge.

Caer flew down to him and took his arm, touching it and the white spotlight finally found them and then another golden one, showed her healing his arm. He bowed in gratitude and flew off.

Then she rose, up into the center of the room, filled with her own strength and glory, only to be almost bowled over by Trina. She recovered. They circled each other threatening and feinting, but unable to touch the other. The music swelled and cascaded and they followed it.

Normally, Caer had no trouble keeping things even with Trina. But today, the buildup of no days off, mingled with the atomizers disfunction, the unusable elevator and having to run up two flights of stairs to make her entrance, along with the wrong size of the performance space caused her to mess everything up.

She couldn't keep up her half.

She was falling behind, which set her off even more. Trina noticed and tried to slow down, as far as the music would allow. Caer began to back off from the battle a music passage too early, tears still streaming down her face from the chilis.

Trina caught the movement and began her own retreat, mirroring Caer.

Caer made it to the tunnel on the fifth floor and went into the dancer's room.

She collapsed on a stool and whispered breathlessly into the com, "Fix the damn atomizers, they're malfunctioning. And Elevator 3 isn't working."

Then she poured herself a cup of water. She had ten minutes. Maybe.

She stood in front of the fans, drenched with sweat and crying. Trying to get all the chili out of her eyes. She gave herself five minutes of that, then blotted her face and reapplied makeup. Then she stretched and left the room, trying to calm herself.

As she passed the elevator, it opened and out came typing man.

"Stay the fuck out of the elevator during the performance," she hissed.

He jumped and looked up from his phone, "Uh, okay."

She continued on into the tunnel, trying to regain a sense of calm and focus.

The air felt clearer now. The music shifted, deep cellos grounded it. Collin appeared, sitting on a huge cliff that jutted out from a wall below.

She floated down to him, trying to help him as he brooded and asked the gods for assistance. Then she began flying in a large circle, joined by the kids. The teenagers, still air dancers in training. They fluttered around in her sunbeam and golden goodness, in a rainbow of colors.

Then, at the appearance of Jeannie, all in royal blue, standing on a cliff across the room, the kids flew offstage. Caer remained hovering above, watching the lovers come together for the first time. Then at the end of the scene, the performance space dimmed, the music trailed off and the dancers went offstage.

Caer flew into a different tunnel on the fifth floor and the audience lights came on. It was the end of Act I.

She went into the dancer's room. Twenty minutes until the next act began. She lay on the floor stretched out on her belly and panting. At least the atomizers were working better. She'd caught the scents of roses and lilies, although she knew that below those hovered the pheromones of love and lust. But she was still overtired. She drank a bit more water and just lay there. Hoping the rest of the show would run more smoothly.

Before she was ready, the voice over the com said, "Places."

And she was off into the tunnel for Act II.

CHAPTER 7 - ANGUS

ANGUS SLUNK TO HIS SEAT IN THE FRONT ROW AFTER HAVING BEEN chastised by the dancer. It hadn't occurred to him the dancers would need the elevators during the performance.

The smell of smoke filled the air. He knew that beneath those lay grief and anger, the effect-aroma used by modern entertainment. It didn't help ease his anxieties.

He'd retreated to the elevator because it was the closest place he could get some solitude to send the various messages in a last ditch attempt to save his company. Still, he felt hopeless about it.

His mouth tasted pasty. Why hadn't he brought a water bottle along?

Angus took several deep breaths. Tried to let go of the tension. He needed to focus on the present.

On her.

He watched the dancer soar through the performance space, her lithe, muscular body the one he'd memorized from his dreams.

Angus felt torn.

He wanted to watch her fly, but he needed to do everything he could to keep the company afloat.

That morning his father had sent him a message. Everything was over.

The Board was shutting down Core Growth Industries.

Killing any buildings still alive. They'd be torn down and the sites rebuilt with conventional buildings.

Angus spent the morning and the first part of the performance sending messages to the Board and to Jonathon, telling him not to kill the building.

He'd gotten no responses back from anyone.

So, there he sat watching her fly, the beauty of her floating in front of him. Her powerful wings made a powerful wind.

And his own life was ruined. Even if he had the nerve to approach her, he had nothing to offer her.

He was currently unemployed with no prospects. Soon, he'd be out of money with no place to live.

And yet. There she was. The woman he'd been dreaming about for an entire year. He couldn't not try to talk to her. She was quite extraordinary.

Angus sat through the Intermission, listening to the music playing the same themes as the first half. Cellos and violins swelling, accented by saxophones, drums and trumpets.

When should he to try to speak with her? And what would he say? Should he tell her about the dreams?

He finally decided to wait until after the performance. The dancers were coming to a reception. He knew she'd be mobbed by people, but he should wait and not interrupt the flow of her performance. Again.

Now, he just had to figure out what to say.

Next to him, Jonas was concentrating on Meredith. He'd given Angus his condolences and that was all he had.

And Father, well, who knew where he was? Probably trying to mop up Angus' mess. Assuring the media that Daddy was stepping in and would see that Core Growth Industries was shut down and cleaned up. Buildings killed and torn down. Reassuring the public that everyone was safe again.

Father was one of the people who hadn't responded to any of his messages. Which was just like him.

Just as intermission ended, the old man came and sat down in his seat, next to Meredith. He nodded at Angus, a dismissive nod.

Nothing had changed then.

Angus took a deep breath and felt his heart sink.

There was no hope for his business life right now.

The thought of the buildings being torn down ripped at his soul. They were alive. Sentient. Their loss would leave a gaping hole in the universe.

Lives that could never be replaced or replicated.

The music started up, the rat-a-tat-tat of the drums followed by the rest of the recorded orchestra. Conflict poured out of the effect-aroma machines. He could see the audience below him go rigid in response. Felt his own anger and antagonism building.

He wanted to hit something. To fight for the lives of the buildings.

Angus watched the air dancers, trying to lose himself in the story, but he couldn't. He'd missed too much of the first half and he couldn't get into the story. Something about two sides warring. And a love affair.

He glanced across the way at the audience and saw Jonathon standing behind the seats.

Why was Jonathon here? He wouldn't been invited. He wasn't high up enough in the company to rate an invitation.

Was Jonathon looking for him? He hadn't answered any of Angus' messages, so probably not.

Did Jonathon know someone else here?

Paranoia began to grip his mind. What if one of the Board Members wanted to get rid of Angus' company? Who would be better to assist with that than Jonathon? He could contaminate the building's original cells. Or mess up the growth process, causing the building to do what it did. Then the building would be brought to the medias' attention.

Angus' mind was still spinning out of control when She dove out of the tunnel next to him. He was so startled, he nearly jumped from his seat.

She twirled and plunged seemingly out of control, then at the last moment, turned upwards and ascended. It both thrilled and terrified him.

What would it feel like to be able to fly like that? He'd love to be able to do that.

She floated close to him. He could feel the gusts caused by her wings, smell her sweat. So close he could touch her. If only he reached out

Her eyes watching the dancer in black. The two dancers began circling each other. Feinting in and out, wingtips brushing as they danced together.

Then Angus' attention was caught by Jonathon. Still standing across the way.

He dropped his coat. Brought a rifle up to his shoulder.

Shot it directly at him. The noise of it going off masked by the drums of the music. Angus saw a small flare come from the gun.

In slow motion, the same moment the gun shot, Angus saw the white dancer fly in front of him. She jerked as the bullet caught her.

Angus yelled, jumped from his seat. Moving towards the aisle between his seat and the dancer's tunnel. Phone on. Security.

He watched her fall. The black dancer dove to catch her. Wasn't strong enough to stop the fall. Just slowed it down. Other dancers swarmed up to help.

Angus looked across the way.

Jonathon was gone.

Chaos took over.

The audience figured out that the dancer had been shot. Real blood gushed from her, looking more fake than the fake blood.

Lights everywhere flashed on. The music stopped. Security showed up en masse.

Even Jonas looked alarmed.

"That was meant for you, wasn't it?" he asked Angus.

"I think so. But I don't know why."

"Who?"

"Jonathon, the Chief Engineer of Core Growth."

Angus tried to excuse himself. He needed to get down to her. To get in the ambulance. To go to the hospital. To see how badly she was hurt.

Security showed up and said, "We need to get all of you to a secure location."

They wouldn't let him go. His last sight was of her struggling body, being taken out of the performance space through one of lower hallways.

Then they ushered his family into the elevator and into security cars and off to a downtown hotel. Angus got a suite to himself and directions from security not to leave. He'd wait a few hours. But not more.

She'd be in surgery probably.

Hopefully.

He couldn't believe that he'd finally found her only to lose her.

He got a message to his Assistant, Alison, who tracked down the hospital the dancer was taken to and a room number. But they wouldn't release any information about her. He'd have to go in person.

Security found the video footage of Jonathon taking the shot. But he'd gotten out of the building before they could catch him. The gun had been plastic, didn't register on the useless metal detectors. There was no word yet on why he'd been let in the building anyway.

Angus took a shower, using the minty smelling hotel soap and changed into the fresh clothes he'd been brought. Jeans and a white T-shirt. He felt numb. He didn't know when he'd wear a suit again. Probably on a job interview. But it wouldn't be a blue one. He was no longer a part of the Corporation.

He ate dinner alone and slept.

Then woke up at 12:40 .m. It was time to go.

He splashed cold water on his face. Drank some tap water, scrunching up his face at the purification chemicals. They tasted awful.

Back out in the main room he sat and pulled on socks and shoes. Ran his fingers through his hair and took his wallet, checking to make sure there was cash in it. And his credit card registered to a different name and account, which no one knew about. At least no one who might be looking for him.

He left his phone on the nightstand. Too traceable and did he really want to talk to anyone who had that number anyway?

He picked up a light jacket, slipping it over his arm. As he walked down the hall, one of the security guards stopped him.

"I can't sleep. I'm just going to the bar and get a couple of drinks. Then I'll come back."

The guard looked skeptical.

Angus knew the man didn't have a reason to doubt him. Angus was known for his honesty. Which was why he'd be able to get away with all this.

"Just be careful. He's still on the loose," said the guard.

"No one knows where we're at, though. Right?"

The guard nodded.

"I'll be careful."

Then he took the elevator to the first floor. Walking to the bar, he looked for security, but saw no one, except the desk clerk. He entered the darkly lit room and sat at a table in the back. The place reeked of stale cigarette smoke and alcohol. Who even smoked these days? Apparently someone did. He ordered an expensive scotch that he charged to his room. Let Spears

Corporation pay for that. No use spending valuable cash until he had to.

Angus finished the scotch slowly, Barely tasting it. He waited a few minutes, long enough for the security cameras to pick him up. Then went to the restroom and put the black jacket on, pulling the collar up around his neck.

He mingled with a group of people leaving the bar and followed them out the hotel door, keeping his face down and hoping the cameras wouldn't pick catch him. He wished he had a hood, it would have helped.

Angus slid into a taxi, just outside the door and had it take him to another hotel, one with less security. He went inside, just long enough to buy a dark green sweatshirt at their gift shop. He put it on with the hood up, went back outside and got in a different cab.

Once inside, he settled in. Where was Jonathon and what was he up to? Why would he try to kill Angus, rather than his father, who made the final decision to pull the plug?

None of this made any sense.

CHAPTER 8 - CAER

AT THE BEGINNING OF ACT II, CAER PLUNGED OUT OF THE TUNNEL. Music was swelling and the atomizers had been adjusted. Conflict filled the air with a haunting scent of longing beneath it. She ignored both.

She had mostly recovered from the mess of the first act. Caer watched as Trina circled around her, light and dark, good vs. evil. They danced, wingtips touching, backed away and came forward again, posturing like peacocks.

Then Caer twisted and began her dive. She barely heard the loud pop, not from the music.

Pain shot through her right side.

Her wing wouldn't respond at all.

Her dive became a fall.

Panic filled her entire being. A loud screaming sound. From her own mouth.

She held out her left wing, spread eagled her legs, trying to slow herself down. Hoping the others would see and come help.

The pain burned through her like a flame.

Trina was there first, grabbing her and trying to slow her.

Others came shooting out of the tunnels, ready to catch her. Wings flapping madly.

Lights flashed on and the music stopped.

Why, why couldn't they go on without her?

Don't stop the show. She didn't want to be the cause of a show being stopped.

Somehow, she was lifted, pulled into the lowest hallway. She found herself walking down the corridor, Trina supporting her and saying, "It'll be okay. You'll be fine."

But she didn't believe it.

Someone wrapped a robe around her and they kept her walking.

Dizzy.

She was shaking and kept repeating, "Please, finish the show."

They couldn't stop the show because of her.

"We'll take care of it," said someone.

Her shoulder still burned and her back felt wet.

Was she bleeding?

At the end of the long, long corridor a security guard opened the door and she was walked, half carried, out to a parking garage. An ambulance pulled up to the door and two medics rushed out.

"What happened?" asked one, as the other took her good arm and pulled her inside the back. They lay her face down on the bed in the ambulance

"We don't know," said Trina. "She might have been shot. Her wing's broken and there's blood everywhere."

The medic took her handprint and did a scan of her eye and checked her medical records.

Caer lay shivering. Why was she so cold?

She felt a blanket cover her lower body.

Everything seemed to be blurred, as if she was watching it and feeling nothing emotionally. Almost as if she was dreaming. No, not dreaming. When she dreamt, she felt everything.

"We need to get her to the hospital," said one of the medics.

"I'm coming along," said Trina.

"No," said Caer. "Finish the show. You have to finish the show."

The medic said, "You can come see her afterwards."

Trina nodded. "You take care of yourself. I'll go see what I can do to get things going again."

"See ya," said Caer.

The medic gave her an injection and she slipped into unconsciousness.

And felt herself falling.

A long fall into a dark abyss. And the abyss was filled with terror and things that haunt the night.

CHAPTER 9 - ANGUS

ANGUS RODE THE ELEVATOR UP TO THE EIGHTH FLOOR. HE HATED hospitals.

This was the old hospital. It had been designed by someone from California. The idea had been to use lots of natural lighting.

However in New Seattle, that meant gray, cloudy skies. They lighting they'd added in when they found it was too dim was still too dark and just looked gloomy. Everyone looked sick.

The awful smell of death and cleaning liquids filled the old elevator, which looked too old to work.

The hood he wore up hid most of his face. He kept his head down, not making eye contact.

He held a bouquet of white roses up to his nose. He'd bought them at the gift shop. They were actually fragrant. It was an extravagant gift for someone who was suddenly unemployed, but he needed to be extravagant right now.

He took another breath mint from his pocket and sucked on it. It would be better to get rid of the scotch smell.

As he stepped off the elevator, he could tell immediately which room was hers. It was surrounded by dancers. Many still in costume. Those out of costume, were dressed to the hilt. Then he remembered the reception that had been planned for after the ballet. Had it still gone on?

He smiled at everyone and squeezed past them, into her room. They glared at him, an outsider. An older man, still in a black costume, stood on the far side of her bed. Two women, the dancer in black and another woman, in regular clothes, who was older, sat and whispered in a corner and looked up when he entered.

He pushed the hood off. There were no cameras in the individual rooms.

Caer lay in the bed, on her side, facing him, eyes closed. Of course, dancers would find it uncomfortable to sleep on their backs with those wings. Her wing was bandaged. But it didn't look like it was enough to fix a broken wing.

"Who are you?" asked the man, quietly.

"I'm Angus Speares. She was directly in front of me when she was shot. I believe that bullet was meant for me," he said.

"I'm John, Caer's father."

Angus nodded at him. Caer, so that was her name. Lovely.

"How is she?"

"Her wing's broken. They're flying in a specialist, but they don't think she'll dance again."

"I'm so sorry. When did she get the surgery?" Angus asked.

John just stared at him.

"When did she get her wings? How old was she?" Angus asked.

"She was born with them," said John.

"I didn't know that was possible."

"She was the first," John said. He turned away and stared out the window.

"Will she fly again?"

John shrugged in response.

The black dancer in the corner asked, "Why was someone trying to shoot you?"

Angus turned to her.

"I'm not sure. He was one of my employees and the company has been shut down by my father. Revenge? I truly don't know."

"So he loses his job and you're home free," said the woman next to her.

The older woman had golden colored wings to match her hair. She wore a sweater and jeans. Somehow, he felt she was the power in the room, but he didn't know her relationship to Caer. Mother? Perhaps. If she was, the woman had no attachment to Caer's father. They barely acknowledged each other.

"Not exactly. My father gave each of us, his two sons, one chance. We each picked a company to run and he gave it to us. To succeed or fail. My brother was a stunning success. Apparently, I've been deemed a failure."

"So what happens to you?" asked the dancer in black.

"I don't know. I'm out of a job. I need to go find another one, just like anyone else. And who's going to hire a failed CEO? Nobody's that foolish these days," he said, his heart sinking. "I have to reinvent myself somehow."

The older woman asked, "What company was it?"

"Core Growth Industries."

"I thought so," she said. "Pity that. I liked the idea of living buildings."

"I did too. I didn't give the order to shut down, but the Board apparently couldn't handle the bad media exposure. I think things would have worked themselves out. That the buildings would have...well, that's all done now. Nothing I can do to change it now."

"Most men in your position wouldn't come to the hospital bed to apologize," the older woman said.

"No probably not. The Family's lawyers will have my head. But my mother taught me to do the right thing. This is the right thing. I can't undo what happened, but I certainly have to acknowledge it."

53

"You know that admitting the bullet was meant for you. it give us ammunition to sue you?"

"Yeah. I know. It wouldn't do you much good, though. I'm not worth suing. My father, or the Board, that's another story. Once I move to a smaller, cheaper apartment, I've got about three months of living expenses to my name. I invested nearly everything I had into Core Growth because I believed in it. I still do, but in retrospect I didn't anticipate the politics involved."

Why was he airing all this faults and failures to this woman, whose name he didn't even know?

"Excuse my, but who are you?" he asked.

"I'm Gillian. Caer's mother."

"And I'm Trina," said the dancer in black. "Caer's friend."

"Do you have any idea when she'll wake?"

"Not for hours they said. They put her under so she won't move her wing. They couldn't really immobilize it. The surgeon should be here about the time she wakes up and then? ..." her mother said, shrugging.

"Well, I'll just leave these," he said, putting the flowers down on a table already covered with flowers. I need to get moving. I'll try to come back when she's awake."

"Are you in trouble?" asked Gillian.

"Probably. They put our family under protection, they know who the shooter is, but he escaped. I snuck out, I needed to see her."

"Are you going back?" asked Gillian.

"If I do, they won't let me escape again, they'll see right through any pathetic attempt I can make. They didn't see the last one coming. And I don't relish spending time with my family at the moment."

"I may be out of line here," said Gillian, "we don't know you and you don't know us, but maybe you should come stay with me. At the Company's space."

"Gillian, you have no right," said John.

"I have every right to invite a guest to stay in my home. I'm a founding member and I don't pull rank often. And you never had the right to tell me what to do, so don't start trying now."

"I don't want to get in the way," said Angus.

Why was she asking him? His brain followed out a paranoid scenario of abduction and hostage taking. No, that didn't make sense.

"You're not in the way. Some people are just incapable of dealing with their own guilt." She glared at John.

John held his hands up in the air in acquiescence.

"Come. I have an extra room. No one will know you're there. I'm going home now, try to get some sleep, so I can come back when she's awake. I want to be here when the surgeon arrives."

"Don't try and argue," said Trina. "Gillian really is in charge of everything at company."

"Okay, you've convinced me."

He put his hood up, took one last look at Caer's pale, but peaceful face and walked the gauntlet of dancers outside the door.

"Jason, Gregor, could you two stay till I get back? I want to make sure she's safe."

"I'd be honored," said a burly man, dressed in black. He wasn't a dancer and had no wings.

"I'll stay," said another, a thickset, muscular dancer with short strong wings. He'd changed after the performance apparently, into a pair of jeans and a wrap shirt styled the same as the other dancers wore. Angus had never even thought to wonder how someone with wings could wear a shirt. The man's skin was dyed gray, probably for the performance.

He followed Gillian to the elevator, which they rode to the basement. She unlocked the doors of a black car which must have been twenty years old. Sitting inside, she punched in a destination. The car was so old it couldn't follow voice commands. The seats were worn and not particularly clean. There was makeup smeared on the plastic seats.

He sat across from her. The car drove off.

"You're probably wondering why I asked you to come with me."

"It had crossed my mind."

"Caer won't dance again. The bones that attach her wing are shattered. And the muscles holding the bones in place have been severed. If they can fix it, she'll be able to move her wings again, maybe even fly. But she won't have the control to dance. And by the time she's regained her strength, she'll be too old for all but the most minuscule of parts. The dance isn't forgiving. She's not the type who will be content with designing and making costumes, like me. She doesn't have enough experience to move into a choreographer's position. There's too much competition. She needs to make a transition to the outer world, before her heart breaks."

"The doctor told you this, even before the surgeon has come?"

"He talked a little about it. But I've seen this kind of damage before. On more seasoned and stronger dancers. It's not good. It may be kinder to remove her wings. That choice will be up to her. But I know my daughter. She loves the dance. She lives for the dance. And to hang around watching others dance, knowing she never will again, that would kill her. Slowly. She needs a way out."

"And what do I have to add to this?"

"I like you. You're kind, ethical and smart. You need a job, a change. I'll pay you to help her find her way out of this."

"I'm not exactly a therapist. If I were, my life wouldn't be such a mess."

"She doesn't need a therapist. Well, she will, but she probably won't accept it. She's bull-headed enough to want to do everything herself. She needs a friend who is from outside. Who understands outside and can help her transition."

"I don't know how useful I'd be. I understand a certain social strata, the one where big money moves. Doesn't mean I navigate it well. But that's where I've lived my whole life. Sheltered from having a real job, from life in the real world. I've lived on my own, out of school, for only three years. I have my own apartment, well, I did. Paid my own bills. But I've never learned how to clean, or cook. I pay for that. I can manage a company, but I haven't a clue how to do normal things, like play with kids, do my own laundry or even shop for clothes."

"I think you'll do fine. She's only been out of our complex a couple dozen times. We keep our young dancers inside. It's too dangerous out in the world for them."

"Why?"

"You are too young to remember the '80's. When the first winged people were made. There were uproars about genetic manipulation in humans. And the process was extraordinarily difficult and agonizing." She shivered and he knew she was remembering the pain. "The first and second generations of winged people were ostracized, bullied and abused. The same was true of water people. Anything or anyone that the great mass of humans can't understand is frightening and therefore must be attacked. Humans haven't changed much in our entire history. It was a witch hunt. Eventually, we were accepted but only after the government decided we were mostly useless to them and we moved into the arts. The arts have always been where outcasts are allowed to live. Because art is brushed aside as unimportant. Even though it's artists who drive society, they move our culture forward towards the light. And the dark."

"I heard about some of the problems, but didn't realize it was so bad."

"Trust me, I lived it. It was. I was created by the government."

He nodded.

They rode across the city in silence. The sun was rising, behind the clouds, but the clouds were heavy and dark, filled with rain to come. The roads were crowded with traffic, like any normal morning.

His life had imploded and what the Board hadn't killed, Angus had probably murdered all on his own.

"Can we stop, at a coffeehouse, for just a moment? I want to tell my family I'm safe. So they'll stop looking for me."

"Sure," she said.

In the next block, she had the car pull over. He jumped out and ran into the shop. He stood in the short line and paid cash for use of their message system.

"Good morning, everyone. I had to leave. I've got things to do and now that I'm without a company, it's time to do them. I just want you to know I'm safe and will get in touch when I've got my life sorted out again. I know that Core Growth was still in the red, even after I sank everything into it. So please have someone sell my apartment, car and anything else worth that's worth money. Donate everything else. Thanks for the opportunity, Father. Sorry I failed you. Angus."

Then he went back to the car. They drove to somewhere on top of the old part of Capital Island. The area had been completely devastated by the big quake of '75. And rebuilt. But it was still a sleazy area of town. Too close to the water to be truly safe. But people crowded there because they could afford it.

"This is it," said Gillian.

The complex looked huge. At least two blocks long and wide. Built all on one large chunk of land with streets that dead ended in the middle of it. No windows facing the streets and built like a prison. Not for keeping people inside though, but for keeping them out. Impregnable.

They turned into an underground parking lot. There was a first gate that was an electronic gate that let them in and then a human guard near the elevator. The car parked itself and they got out and walked to the elevator. The car apparently didn't have drop off capability. Old cars were like that.

"Well hello Gillian, how's Caer?"

"It's too soon to tell Emiel. It's not looking good right now."

"Well, I sure hope she pulls out of it."

"Me too. This is Angus, he'll be staying with us, although no one outside is to know."

"Hello Angus, and welcome."

"Hello. And thanks."

They got into the industrial looking elevator and sped upwards. Then walked for what seemed like two blocks through a warren of tall, wide hallways obviously meant to accommodate dancers' wings.

The hallways were decorated in wild colors, some of them had murals painted on walls. Old patched carpet lined the floor. Obviously when a stretch became too worn, it was taken out and another piece with a completely different pattern was laid down. Many of the doors were decorated with the occupant's name and masks or feathers.

He could smell curry and coffee wafting down the hall. It made his stomach rumble. When had he eaten last? Yesterday? The day before?

Gillian's apartment was at the far end of the long hall. Her door was completely bare. No name and no design.

Which he guessed meant that everyone knew her.

She unlocked the door with her palm and they entered.

To his new life.

Which would be what?

CHAPTER 10 - CAER

CAER FELT GROGGY. AS IF WAKING FROM A DEEP DREAM. SHE'D BEEN falling. Her wing was broken.

She heard voices and gradually was able to pry her eyes open. But things were still foggy.

It smelled strange. Sterile and flowery all at the same time. And she smelled sweat. The room felt warm, warmer than the dancers' quarters. Warmer than a rehearsal space.

She wore a baggy nightgown that was open at the back. Her skin felt chalky, like when she sweated and it dried on her. She hadn't showered.

Her vision cleared more and she saw Gillian listening to a woman wearing a white coat. She saw pale green walls, sea green. And she was lying on her side in a hospital bed, her wings tied down with a bandage that wrapped around her chest. She couldn't move them.

Her mouth felt dry. So very dry.

Then she noticed him. A lovely man sat in a chair next to her bed. He sat staring at her, saying nothing and seemed to be waiting. She gazed into his deep blue eyes and felt a kinship there.

Caer knew immediately that she could trust this man.

Gillian turned and said, "Honey. You're awake.

The doctor looked at her, staring into her eyes. Probably checking the pupils to see if they were the same size.

Didn't doctors do stuff like that? Caer knew she'd fallen.

Had she hit bottom?

"I'm awake," she croaked.

"Here let me get you some water, don't move," said Gillian. She handed her a water bottle with a straw in it. Caer took a sip of the water, moving as little as possible. Why did her wing hurt so much?

"What happened?" she asked.

"You were shot during the performance. During the pas de deux with Trina. You fell, she pulled up on you, kept you from falling as quickly. So did the other dancers. You never hit the floor," said Gillian.

"Where did I get shot? And who shot me? Why would anyone do such a thing?"

She couldn't remember the performance.

"The bullets hit you right in the joint where your wing joins your shoulder," said the woman in the white coat.

"As to why," said the man. "that was my fault. I'm afraid I was the intended victim. You got in the way of the bullet."

She looked at him again. He seemed familiar. Then she remembered seeing him, rumpled suit, typing messages on his phone.

"You're the typing man."

His eyebrows raised.

"During the performance you were typing in your phone. Sending messages? You held up the elevator when I was trying to get to my place. I had to run up flights of stairs."

"Yeah, that was me. I really screwed up that day, huh? I'm sorry. I was so wrapped up in my life exploding, I wasn't really paying attention to anyone else."

"I dealt with it, I guess. My performance would have been turned around. If I hadn't gotten shot. Did you finish the show?" she asked Gillian.

"Yes dear, you told Trina that it was important. We made an announcement and started the act over again with Maria in your place and Jenny in hers. Everything worked out, but Maria isn't as graceful as you. I missed your performance."

Caer didn't say anything for a bit. She just let things sink in a few minutes.

Then she asked, "Why are my wings tied down?"

"Are you ready to talk about this?" asked the doctor. "I'm Dr. Cosby. I've worked quite a bit for the London Aerial Ballet. I'm a wing specialist."

"I'm ready. It's not good news, is it?"

"I'll be honest with you. No. It's not. Your joint is shattered. We have two options, but it's possible that neither will work. It's possible that you might never fly again. And if you can, it's highly unlikely you'll ever dance again. I've never see such damage to a joint before. It would be kinder to remove your wings altogether. And I'm not saying that lightly, but you deserve the truth."

Caer winced.

Someone might as well cut her heart out.

"The first choice is to glue your joint back together, making artificial pieces if we need to. That will be a long and complicated procedure. It will take a long time to heal. The second alternative is to make an artificial joint and insert it. That's what they used to do when the government first made flyers. Our technology has improved since then, so some of the issues people had back then, probably won't come up for you. It would be a simpler, faster operation."

"But which one will give me the best chance of flying again?" asked Caer.

"If, and it's a big if, your body accepts the artificial joint, your chances with either would be equal. There are no viable tests which will tell us in advance. The tests for other artificial body parts simply don't work on wings and bone strengthening solutions. Part of the reason why the government stopped the program. Making humans flyable is hard work."

"So, if everything goes well the choices will have the exact same result. But if my body rejects the artificial joint, then the first one be the better choice? There'll be no difference in my ability to fly?"

The Dr. Cosby sighed. "There would be a small difference. The artificial joint would require you to adapt to it. We've never had a person who was born winged who had to switch to one. Remember, you're the first. But for flyers who had original artificial joints that needed replacing, the new artificial joints require some time to get used to. It won't work as smoothly as the one you were born with."

"So, why can't I dance again?" asked Caer.

"You're twenty, right?"

"Eighteen, Caer said.

"To put your joint back together will take several surgeries. Spaced out over a few weeks. Then you'll need time for rehab. I'd be surprised if you were able to fly before three years. We'll have to cut through a few muscles and some of yours are already severed. There'll be scar tissue. It will take you years of strengthen those muscles enough to just get you off the ground. You'll be in your late twenties before you'd be able to be strong enough to have some grace in the air. And that's if everything goes well and you heal quickly. If it doesn't and you don't, add a couple years to that. So early thirties before you can even think about being good enough to perform a small role that doesn't require much effort. How many dancers do you think you'll be up against for that role? If everything heals perfectly and you're able to regain your strength to where you are now, you'll still be in your late twenties, early thirties, competing for roles with dancers in their early twenties, who haven't had to take years off. They'll be a decade ahead of you. I've seen dancers destroyed by accidents like this. Nothing will ever be the same for you. Like I said, it would be kinder to remove both your wings and for you to take that drive and use it to start a new life. Think about it. It is an option."

"I don't think I could live with that. I was born with wings for a reason," Caer said, gritting her teeth. Anger seethed deep inside her.

"You've got a day or two to make a decision. I'll be heading back to London in a week. I'll check in this evening to see how you're doing." She nodded and left the room.

"Caer, you don't have to give up dancing," said Gillian.

"Mom, I just want to be alone."

Gillian nodded and touched Angus' arm. He nodded at her as she went out the door.

"I know you don't know me and I'll leave in a minute. I came for two reasons. The first to apologize."

"You didn't shoot me."

"No, but it was one of my employees who shot you. I feel somehow responsible. I needed to come apologize. I know now that nothing I can say about that will matter. But I just wanted to let you know that I'll be here to help. Every day."

"Just because the bullet was meant for you? You don't owe me anything."

"No, it's because of the second reason. But I think you've probably been given enough to think about for one day."

That only made her madder.

"Don't coddle me."

"I'm not. I just want to get to know you better before I tell you more. And I think you probably need to focus on your future. I'm trying to help, in my own clumsy way."

"I'm sorry. I'm being rude. I'm pissed off about my lack of future and not fit to talk to."

"You don't have a lack of future. It just looks like a pretty rocky one, no matter which path you choose," he said. "Sort of like my own."

"That's an understatement. Someday, once I've come to a decision, maybe you can tell my why your future looks as rocky as mine."

"Perhaps. Maybe by then, something will have shaken loose. Who knows? Well, I'll leave you alone to think. I'll come back this afternoon. See if you're in the mood to talk."

She nodded and watched him leave.

Who was he and what did he want from her?

She felt confused about everything. And it wasn't from the pain meds.

Her whole life, which had been so clear, was now in complete disarray.

Cut her wings off?

Never fly again?

That wasn't possible. If that was the case, then why had she been the first human born with wings?

CHAPTER 11 - ANGUS

ANGUS SAT IN GILLIAN'S APARTMENT, AT HER ANTIQUE OAK DINING table. She had few belongings and her rooms were tastefully decorated in white. Minimalism. That's what it was called.

He sipped a black tea grown in Oregon out of a white tea cup. The strong round flavor of it mellowed a bit by cream. Real cream. She was tidying up the kitchen and had refused his help.

Apparently, the dancers ate nearly all their meals in the communal dining room, but most of the apartments had small kitchens for snacks. Dancers ate an astonishing amount of food. But then they did harder physical work than he'd ever seen.

Gillian had a screen on and when Angus heard the headlines and his jaw dropped open with disbelief.

Jonathon had been caught. And he confessed 'everything', telling the media he'd been hired by Angus to kill his father. That Angus' anger at his father, for shutting down Core Growth Industries, was insatiable. He planned to kill the Board members one by one.

There was a clip from his father, expressing regret over his son's actions. Someone asked what was happening with Core Growth and Jonas came forward. He'd been assigned to deal with

Core Growth and deciding which programs to wrap up and which to move forward on.

Jonas smiled his billion dollar smile for the camera. Angus had tried not to pay attention to how much of a pompous ass his brother was.

Jonas said, "We've found there are indeed some interesting things happening with the latest building. It's reinventing the electrical, plumbing and communication systems in a more efficient manner than humans have ever considered. We feel it's important to study these innovations and see if they are applicable to our future building programs. It's one of the biggest discoveries humans have made. Our world has been looking up into the skies since the dawn of time, wondering and waiting to find other life in the universe and now we've created it right here on Earth. I'll keep you abreast of what we're finding. No more questions right now, please. Our family is grieving the loss of a son and brother."

The announcer noted that Angus Spears was missing and that when found would be arrested for attempted murder of his father, and conspiring to commit assault with a deadly weapon. Then vids of him were plastered all over the screen.

He buried his head in his hands.

"I know you didn't do it," said Gillian, now sitting across from him. "But what are you going to do about it?"

"I don't know. There's never been a lot of love coming from the old man or my brother, but I never thought they'd do this to me."

"Are you sure they are guilty of what you're thinking they did? Isn't it this man, Jonathon's fault. He could have lied to them."

"No, probably not. It's not a coincidence that Jonas is taking over my company and making the same 'world changing' discoveries that I did. No, all this was a ploy to steal my company right out from under me. And I was stupid to trust them. At least Jonas and Jonathon. I've been played and good."

"So, what next?"

"I don't know. I change everything about me and lie low until I figure something out."

"Oh good, a makeover. Shirley's been so bored!"

"Shirley?"

"Our makeup artist. We'll get Aria to do something with your hair and I'll collect clothes for you. By the time we're finished with you, your own family won't recognize you and neither will the cameras! You'll be able to go anywhere."

"I don't believe you can change me that much."

"Ha! Just wait." She spoke to her message system and listened.

Then Gillian said to him, "We're going now. Shirley's got an hour before dress rehearsal makeup starts."

Angus shrugged his cooperation. If they could disguise him, that would be a start at least.

He wasn't sure what it was a start on though.

They left Gillian's apartment and wove through the maze that ran through the dancers' residences. Crossing a sky bridge with three sides encased in glass he saw the gray sky outside. Rain pounded on the glass making him feel exposed and vulnerable.

His heart felt as ashen as the sky at the betrayal of his family. He'd been foolish to trust them, thinking that blood was that thick, at least. His mother would have been appalled if she was alive.

Angus really had lost everything. He felt empty and disoriented.

He followed Gillian past the performance spaces, rehearsal rooms, props, costuming and stopped at makeup.

Inside two women waited, drinking coffee from steaming mugs. Shirley was a tall, plump redhead with no wings. Aria, a brunette had short, stubby wings which looked as if they wouldn't support even her small frame.

The room smelled of scented makeup or perfume or something.

They guided him to a chair and set to work.

"Is this how you usually wear your hair?" asked Aria.

"Yeah, I sometimes put product on it to make it lie down more."

"And do you ever wear a beard?"

"No, I just don't have a razor right now."

Shirley said, "Keep the stubble. Let it grow into a beard. We'll need to dye your irises. Brown. And need to hide this space right here." She put her finger on the space be between his eyes, above his nose and just below the eyebrows.

"Why there?" he asked.

"It's the spot the cameras grab to start identifying people's faces. Old, old tech. But it still works mostly, so they use it. How about a long swath of hair for there?" asked Shirley.

"I can match his hair," said Aria. "Put an extension on until his own grows out.

"And I'll need to deepen or lighten shadows in the eye sockets and cheekbones. Pity the beard doesn't come up a bit higher, but we'll make it work. We could do a temporary tattoo on the cheekbone," Shirley looked at him, questioningly.

"I'll leave it up to you," he said.

"The vids always showed you in suits, looking very conservative. Did you ever wear anything else in public or private," asked Gillian.

"In my own apartment, sure. In public, probably not."

"Good, that'll make it easier. I think we should go with high fashion. That way he can tag along and be part of a dancer entourage and fit in," said Gillian.

"Oooh, this is going to be fun," said Aria. "Okay, wash and cut first. Then I'll do the extensions while Shirley's dying your irises."

"Let's go for a deep purple instead of brown," said Shirley.

"I'll go round up some clothes," said Gillian. "I'll be back before it's time to go back to the hospital."

Angus gave himself up to Aria and Shirley, listening to their gossip about the Company. He noticed they avoided the subject of Caer, although he wasn't sure why. If they just didn't want to talk about her in front of him or if it was every dancer's nightmare to lose the function of their wings.

He needed to focus on his next step. What did he need to do?

Should he search for proof that Jonas, and possibly his father, stole the company from him?

And what would he do with it if he found it?

Should he take the data on the company to a competitor? He couldn't do anything out in the open if he was still a suspect in the assault and attempted murder.

Or should he just walk away from that life completely?

His mind felt like fog on a crisp, fall morning. He couldn't see around him. All he could think about was Caer and the horrible position she was in. No one should have to make such a decision.

That path was clear. He needed to stay with her. To support her in whatever way he could. Her life had just turned to hell. And even though he didn't know her at all, he loved her. It was simple. He would stay.

The rest of his life would gain clarity with time.

Time was something he had plenty of for now.

CHAPTER 12 - CAER

CAER LAY IN THE HOSPITAL BED ON HER SIDE. SHE WANTED TO SIT up, but with her wings pinioned, she could only lie or stand. She rolled onto her belly, but that was just as uncomfortable.

She wasn't used to such inactivity. She slid off the bed and stood. The floor felt cold, so she slipped her feet into the felted blue slippers Gillian had brought.

She wanted to go home.

To have her life back the way it was, instead of being prisoner in the hospital. In this pastel peach colored room filled with antiseptic smells. Being woken up several times a day and night so the nurses could check her vitals. Awful, tasteless food. Even their mint tea was weak and grassy tasting. Too old.

Mostly she wanted to move her wings. She wanted to be whole. Not broken.

Caer wanted not to have to make such an awful decision.

She walked to the window, gazing out at the view of New Seattle. The hospital overlooked the mass of buildings that was downtown. Not a tree or natural thing in sight. Not that there'd been any before downtown was built there. It was before her time, but she'd been told that the big quake had leveled everything. Nothing left but rubble.

Just like her life.

She heard rustling behind her and turned. Dr. Cosby.

"You're up, well good afternoon."

"Hello. I've made my decision."

"And…"

"I'm keeping my wings. Even if I can't fly. I want to have the joint reassembled. Not an artificial one."

"Okay. If you're up for it, I'll schedule the first surgery for tomorrow."

"Will I be able to get my wings unpinioned afterwards?"

"Your good one, probably. The broken one, we'll see, but I doubt it."

"One is better than none. It's hard to sit."

"I'll try to schedule the surgeries as close together as possible. It will depend on what your body can take and how fast you heal. You're young, so…" the Dr. shrugged.

"Is there anything I can do to help the healing?" Caer asked.

"I'll give you a list of supplements. And do what I tell you, when I tell you. And find yourself something fun to distract yourself with. For years. Put it out of your head that you'll dance again. Later on, when the surgeries are done and you're strong enough to train and fly, then you can revisit that dream. But for now, come up with a new one."

Caer nodded.

What new dream would that be? She'd never considered a life without dancing.

"Well, I'd better go get you on the schedule. I'll see you tomorrow, although you'll be out." The Dr. went out the door.

Caer went back to staring out the window. How did one go about finding a new life?

Gillian did it once. When she got too old to dance.

Caer would have to ask her mother how she chose. The world

was a huge place. Surely there was a life out there for her to create while she healed.

She heard voices in the hallway and into her room walked Gillian with a man who looked familiar somehow, but she couldn't place him.

"Well, good to see you out of bed," said Gillian, coming up to Caer and hugging her carefully.

"Hi Mom."

"I think you remember Angus, actually, he's Alan now."

Caer looked at him again. This couldn't be the same man. Purple, white and deep blue hair, cut at an angle in the front so that the bangs formed a shade covering half of one eye and the other one completely. The eye that was showing was purple, deep purple, not blue. A pierced ear with a small silver ring through it. His visible cheek showed a temporary, or perhaps permanent tattoo of a winged human flying. A beautifully done tattoo in purple, black and indigo. A loose fitting blue shirt that looked trendy, slacks and shoes. He wore a silver charm bracelet on his wrist, the kind that was currently fashionable. And a small bag around his neck and over one shoulder. He carried himself differently. With more confidence. Not the same man she'd seen at the performance, with the frumpy suit and the air of panic about him.

"You can't be," she said.

"I am," he said.

"How?"

"Shirley and Aria and I did a makeover," said Gillian. "He needed to be hidden. Become someone else."

"Okay, well, how do you like your new look?" asked Caer.

"I'm not sure yet. My old self would never in a million years look like this. And I understand needing to wear the disposable gloves, they're common now and don't leave DNA or prints, but I've never like them," he said, holding up his hands.

"We were going to have him grow a beard, but after the

haircut and extensions and dye, we decided clean shaven was best," said Gillian. "I think he looks gorgeous. Best makeover they've done yet."

"Yes, you do look gorgeous," said Caer. "You fit in with all the dancers and their followers now."

"Well, that's where I'm going to stay for some time," he said.

"Have you made your decision yet?" asked Gillian.

"Yes," said Caer. She folded her arms. "The Dr. was just in and I told her I wanted my original joint reconstructed. She's scheduling a surgery tomorrow."

Gillian nodded. "I thought that would be your choice."

"I don't know if it's the right one."

"There is no right choice, but I think it's the best one for you."

"She also told me that I needed to come up with a new dream for my life. Something fun to distract myself with. I don't know how to do that. My whole life has been about dancing. I don't know what else even exists," said Caer.

"I can help with that," said Angus. "I've seen a lot of life and now that I can go out in public again, I can take you out exploring. When you're ready."

"What do you mean go out in public again?"

"The police think I was behind the attempted murder and the assault on you."

"Were you?" asked Caer.

"No," he said clenching his fists.

"Good. Because I rather like you and if you tried to kill me that would put a crimp in our friendship."

He smiled a little.

"So you're a wanted man," said Caer.

"Yeah."

"Well, I don't know how long after the surgery before I can go out. Or even if I'll be able to until after I've had several. I'm not going anywhere until I can sit down, I'd guess."

"I guess that's a drawback of having wings," he said.

"Yeah. But I'm not giving them up. That would be like cutting off an arm. Even if I can never really use them again."

There were more voices in the hallway and Trina, Johanna and Ginny came in the door. They were loaded down with flowers and bags.

"Good afternoon gorgeous," said Trina, carefully hugging Caer. "We brought you some pick me ups."

Trina dumped her bags on the bed and handed Johanna a bundle of white daisies and white roses and said, "You should ask a nurse for some vases probably."

Johanna laid her bags down and took the flowers, along with Ginny's yellow lilies out the door. Ginny began opening her bags and pulling out packages, arranging them on the tray that sat next to the bed.

A wave of exhaustion swept over her and Caer leaned on the window sill.

Gillian was chatting with Ginny and Trina, helping them unpack.

Angus looked at her and said, "You look pale. Do you need to lie down?"

"I think so. I'm so tired of lying down though."

"You'll be able to sit again. Either that or we'll have to design a special chair for you. You go lie down and I'll go see if the nurses can find a stool for you. We'll see if that will work."

Caer walked back to the bed and pulled back the covers. She climbed in and lay on her side, facing the tray, which was completely covered with beautifully wrapped packages.

"It's like Christmas," she said.

Trina smiled at her.

"I can't lie down and open presents. You'll have to open them for me," said Caer.

"Nope," said Johanna. "You can open one every day, when you stand up. Cause this'll have to last you. We blew our entire paychecks on you."

"You shouldn't have done that," said Caer.

"Aw c'mon," said Ginny. "Friends take care of other friends. If you're going to go through hell, you might as well be entertained."

Angus reappeared carrying a stool, which he set down at the end of the bed. He sat down on it. And watched her. Which made Caer feel self conscious.

Who was he really? What did he want and why was he staying with Gillian? Other than he was hiding from the cops. He must be rich, he could go anywhere. So, why stay here?

His new look only deepened his mysteriousness. He fascinated her. And the makeover only highlighted his eyes and those cheekbones. She found it hard not to stare at him.

She noticed Trina couldn't take her eyes off him either. At least Ginny and Johanna were making an effort. Gillian was standing behind them, taking it all in, amusement sparkling through her eyes as she met Caer's eyes. Her mom loved to stir things up.

But Caer noticed that Angus wasn't paying much attention, other than being polite, to anyone but her. His gaze filled her with warmth. His attention made her feel safe in a way she hadn't felt since she was seven and formally moved out into the world of the dance. She'd been dancing since she could walk and fly, but at seven she began to take things seriously.

Perhaps this shelter he provided would allow her to have a place from which she could create a new dream for her life.

Perhaps.

CHAPTER 13 - ANGUS

ANGUS SAT IN THE CAER'S LIT HOSPITAL ROOM. SHE'D JUST COME out of surgery and would be out for hours. She lay there, pale even in the dim light, but peaceful looking. The white sheets, her white hair, the white bandages and her skin nearly matching them. The surgery had taken hours and hours. Gillian had finally gone home to sleep.

He sipped from a bottle of lime flavored sparkling water. It fizzled up his nose and he wiped it off. He should probably go find some dinner. There was a barbecue takeout restaurant down the street. He could bring it back here and eat.

Two shadows in the doorway. In walked men in uniform. Cops.

Angus' muscles tightened, ready to run. He knew they weren't here for him. There was no way for them to know that he'd be here. Was there?

"Is this Caer Hayes, the air dancer?"

"Yes. She just got out of surgery. She won't be conscious for hours they told me. Can I help you gentlemen?"

"I'm Detective Midway and this is Detective Kelly. And you are?"

"I'm Alan Johnson, a friend of hers."

"Well Mr. Johnson, we wanted to ask her a couple of questions about the shooting."

"Ah, well I guess you'll have to do it later. She's not going anywhere."

"Were you there at the performance."

"No. I'm just a hanger-onner and I wasn't on the guest list, since it was private. I didn't see her until she was already here."

"Has she talked about what happened?"

"A little, I'm not sure she remembers much. Other than falling. It's something all air dancers are afraid of. Is there something in particular that you want to know about?" asked Angus.

"We're just collecting information. Gotta dot those i's and cross those t's. We don't want to leave any loose ends," said Detective Kelly.

"So, I saw on the news that you think that guy did it to kill his dad?"

"We're still collecting information. That's what the family has said. We've learned not to draw conclusions so early in the investigation," said Detective Midway.

"But didn't him disappearing like that sort of put the nail in the coffin? I mean why would he run away if he wasn't guilty?"

"Not necessarily," said Detective Kelly. "Perhaps he fled because he knew he'd be accused. Perhaps he really was the target and was afraid. You're certainly interested in this, Mr. Johnson."

Was that true? Were they really keeping an open mind about this and not completely believing his family, or was this just their public face?

Angus shrugged, "I watch a lot of mystery/detective vids. I like to try and figure them out, Guess the endings. I sure hope you get whoever did this. It's ruined her career. The doctor said she probably won't ever dance again. Maybe not even fly again."

"I'm sorry to hear that," said Detective Midway. "I love watching air dancers. They're extraordinary."

"Yes, they are," said Angus.

"Well, we'll check back later to talk with her. Thank you."

Angus nodded.

They left the room and he could hear their footsteps echo in the quiet hallway.

He took a deep breath and relaxed a bit.

Caer moaned quietly and he walked to the head of the bed and took one of her soft hands.

"It's okay. Everything's going to be okay. We'll both find our way out of this mess together. You'll find a new life, with me hopefully. And I'll clear my name and be with you. It'll all work out," he said, with a surety he didn't feel.

She had taken her first step, the first surgery. He didn't know where his first step was. Didn't even know which direction to face. He needed information and had no way of getting it. He'd have to hire someone to do it for him.

He switched on the screen in the hospital room and punched in a news channel.

"In other news today, the Old Earth Alliance group are picketing the Core Growth Industries newest project, the building out of control. They say it's dangerous and should be torn down.

The company claims the building is still alive and will remain so because of the valuable research information it is providing. Clearly, many people are very angry about this decision."

Then the news cut to interviews with the people picketing. He turned off the screen.

So, things were heating up out there. He felt sad at the people's misunderstanding of the building process, relieved that their anger wasn't directed at him and a small amount of joy that it was directed towards his brother.

Angus pulled out his phone and skimmed through

advertising sites, looking for a contact number. Finally, he found what he was looking for and tapped it.

"Good afternoon," said a voice that sounded like it had had a rough previous night.

"Hello, is Otis Jackson there?" Angus said, knowing full well that's who'd answered the phone.

"Speaking." There was coughing on the other end of the line.

"Otis, you once did some work for me and I'd like your help again."

"Might be able to help you. Who are you?"

"I'm assuming that you will keep my identity confidential."

"That's how I work."

"I'll pay you more to keep it that way than anyone who might pay you to tell them you found me. Please keep that in mind."

"Oookaaay."

"This is Angus Speares."

Otis whistled, then said, "What can I do you for?"

"I need information. I assume you've been listening to the news."

"Hard to miss."

"Well, I didn't hire Rodriguez to shoot anyone. He was the Chief Engineer of the building. I'm guessing he took the shutdown of the building by the Board hard. Really hard. I thought he was trying to shoot me. Then Jonas took over my company and suddenly I've been accused of setting up the shooting. I need information on what really happened and why."

"Okay. I'll see what I can find out. You know my rates?"

"I'll see that a deposit is made in your account this afternoon. Send me the account number. To this number. I'm no longer using the old one."

"Anything else you want to add to your story?"

"I believe Jonas, and perhaps my father are at the root of all this. The Board told me to shut everything down. Even after I gave them the same story Jonas must have. Unless there have been new developments at the building. Which is possible. I don't know why the Board changed their mind. Maybe they have more confidence with Jonas heading the company. Maybe. I don't quite understand how this all happened, but I do want to know if someone hired Rodriguez to kill me."

"Okay. I'll dig up what I can. And I'll keep in mind your offer about paying more than anyone else who wants you found, but I don't think that'll be necessary. If they're trying to kill you, they've already hired someone to find you."

"I'm lying low," said Angus.

"Good, keep your head down and out of sight. I'll be in touch."

Angus walked to the window and looked out at the leaden colored vista. In the distance, past the downtown of New Seattle, lay what used to be old downtown Seattle. Piles of rubble covered with years of moss and scraggly small plants rose above the water. Makeshift rafts and boats floated between the piles. Trees tried to grow, but the floaters down there chopped them up into firewood. They scavenged wood from the buildings to burn and repair their rafts. Every now and then they moved to a new pile and took everything worth selling, leaving the rest. There were still floors and floors of buildings left untouched even though the big quake had happened twenty-five years ago. A few buildings were partly standing and provided stable homes for the floaters during storms, broken windows boarded up to keep out drafts. There was always smoke coming from there, even on rain-soaked days like this.

He turned to look at Caer. He still dreamt about her every night. It was clear to him that they were meant to be together. But it would take some time and some finesse. She was going to be spending a lot of her time on pain meds. And struggling with her body to heal and grow stronger. Trying to find a new life for herself.

He needed to make sure that life included him.

LINDA JORDAN

Somehow.

CHAPTER 14 - CAER

CAER MANAGED TO STAND, STAGGERING SLIGHTLY FROM THE dizziness. She reached for the hospital provided water bottle and drank the stale water. It was better than nothing.

She leaned on the wall and looked out the window. It was raining outside. And dark. It could have been dawn, or dusk. The old round clock on the wall read 7:26., a.m. or p.m.?

The hallway was busy, people bustling or wandering around. Could be either.

When she woke last night, had it been last night, the nurse had pumped more pain meds into her. Her shoulder and wing joint ached and was tied down.

But her other wing was free. She stretched it out, feeling the stiffness. She knocked some of her gifts on the floor and pulled her wing back in.

This room was cramped. She'd be glad to get out of it. To go home. The dancers' quarters were larger, less cluttered. Wings took up a lot of space.

Bright light suddenly shone in the window. The sun was out.

Caer shook her head, trying to clear it. She didn't want to sleep any longer. How could anyone in this part of the world sleep when the sun came out. It didn't happen that often, especially at this time of year.

She could almost smell the fresh air. Almost.

Instead there was the stale, recycled air of the hospital and the smell of antiseptics. Everything had to be kept so clean here. Even after the superbug scares.

They still used antiseptics. At least in hospitals. Hadn't they learned anything?

She tried walking a bit, the machine her tubes were attached to followed along, but the dizziness was really strong. She had to hold onto the bed, or she would have fallen.

A nurse walked in the door.

"Oh, you're out of bed. We didn't expect you up this soon. Can I get you something?"

"I don't know."

"How are you feeling?"

"Dizzy."

"Are you feeling any pain?"

"No."

"Well maybe the Dr. will let us decrease your meds. I'll talk to her, but I think you need to get back in bed. I don't want you to fall."

"Is it okay if I just sit up for a while. I'm so tired of lying down."

"Okay," the nurse said, scooting the stool over for her. "But be very careful. The meds you're on are making you drowsy. I don't want you to fall asleep and slide off the stool. If you start to feel sleepy, get back in bed. If you need help, pull on the lever. All right?"

"Okay, I'll do that."

The nurse helped Caer sit on the stool and left the room. It didn't feel much better than lying down.

She wanted to walk, but was tethered to the machine which

dripped fluids into her. It would follow her, but it wouldn't support her. She really was too dizzy.

And all she could think of was Angus. No Alan. She was supposed to call him Alan. He'd been there last night, when she woke. Sat and talked to her until she fell back asleep.

Why was he here?

What did he want again?

Her mind felt muddled.

He was here to help her find a new dream. That was it. She needed to figure out something to do with her life.

Caer got up and crawled back into bed, rolling over onto her belly and trying not to get strangled by all the tubes. She'd be glad when the surgeries were all over. Then she could begin to rebuild her life. Into whatever form it was going to take.

All she had now were annoying questions.

CHAPTER 15 - ANGUS

A NGUS SAT IN THE DIMLY LIT CAFE ON M ERIDIAN I SLAND, WHICH was the home of the University. The old University was completely underwater. After the quake, it had been rebuilt on this island. The cafe smelled of coffee and marijuana smoke. It was about half full of students from the University. Some studying and others just hanging out, enjoying the ambience of smoke and candlelight. The sound system played quietly, music from India he guessed.

Angus sipped his bitter coffee. He was here because if his phone wasn't secure, he'd rather the cops find him here than at the dancers' quarters. Or the hospital. It was a new phone, but he knew nothing was ever really secure.

He punched in the number and Otis' deep voice answered.

"Hullo."

"Hi Angus here. You left a message for me to call you."

"Sure. I've got some info for you. I've got a man inside and he talked to Rodriguez. He was trying to kill you. First Rodriguez claimed it was because you shut the company down. You knuckled under. Then, with more persuasion, he said Jonas promised him a job as Vice President in charge of Project

Development. So basically, Rodriguez was in it for the status, the increase in power and of course the money."

"Jonas would never have given it to him."

"You and I know that, but apparently Rodriguez didn't."

"Why didn't Jonas just hire a professional?"

"This way worked out pretty good for him, didn't it? He almost got rid of you and he's disabled Rodriguez. Rodriguez was union, so it would have taken the Earth moving before Jonas could fire him. Now, he can bring in his own team to work on the building. People he trusts."

"Okay, so maybe he didn't want to kill me, just steal the company. Anything else?"

"Yeah, I got an engineer on their staff to talk to me. He wasn't happy with Jonas. Didn't believe all the rubbish Rodriquez threw out. He rather liked you and saw through all the BS. He told me that Jonas has the two buildings locked down tight. Only three of the biological engineers are able to go in. Mostly, Jonas is bringing in politicians and board members. Clearly trying to sell something. All the other engineers are being encouraged to take vacation time or move to another project. There's a lot of grumbling since most of them are only trained or want to work on living buildings. That's their passion. So they're blaming Jonas for all this. Got a few of these guys in a bar together and I learned a lot."

"Such as?" asked Angus.

"The building is still doing new and wonderful things. First, it's apparently resuscitated the older one next to it. Together, they've created a communication center that's beyond anything humans have dreamed. The rumor going around, and it is just rumor, that the center is capable of picking up signals from deep space and that's just the tip of the iceberg. No sign of any signals yet, but only one of the engineers I spoke with was still employed. The buildings seem to be able to work better than our best communication satellites. Core Growth might have had specific plans for the buildings, but apparently the buildings have their own agenda. And we have no idea what that is. And of course, you're getting blame for everything going wrong, at least from management, and Jonas is getting credit for everything that's going right and anything that's innovative."

"Not surprising. I'd do the same thing in his shoes."

"You wouldn't attempt to have your brother killed."

"No, probably not. But at this point, it's tempting."

"Well, that's what I've got so far. You'll have a tough time proving any of this, but I'll contact you when there's more."

"Thanks Otis."

"My pleasure."

Angus didn't linger in the cafe. He went outside in the cold rain and hailed a water taxi over to Upper Fremont. Lower Fremont used to be a historical section of town, but with the big quake and global warming, it was now underwater.

Twenty minutes later, the taxi tied up at the Fremont Dock. Angus got out and walked around getting soaked in the cold rain and stopping at a small restaurant. He dined on heavily spiced black beans and rice. Then he took another water taxi back over to Capital Hill and got out. The rain had stopped and he walked through puddles for several miles to an overlook of the Flats.

It wasn't close to the building, but it was as close as he wanted to get. No one would be looking for him up here. The wind whipped his hair around and he had to hold it back to see.

The new building had grown. It now had a bluish cast and the old one a green. They were visibly connected on several levels and at the top they twined together like two vines reaching for the sun.

What were the buildings up to? They were clearly conscious. But what did that mean? All plants were conscious. This was different, much more complicated.

Dusk approached and the lights at the tips of the buildings began blinking. A safety feature as a warning for low flying aircraft and the occasional flying car. The buildings themselves were lit up completely, running on solar power and the energy of their own liquids, which would circulate as long as the buildings remained alive.

The wind picked up more and Angus shivered, despite his jacket. He should get back to the hospital. Caer's visitors would be leaving for dinner. He could be alone with her.

The doctor was right. The surgeries drained her. She was an athlete in prime shape, but the operations left her completely exhausted. Or perhaps it was the pain and her meds attempting to dull the agony which Caer tried not to let on that she felt.

But he could see it.

She was recovering slowly and hopefully the surgeries were over. Now it was time for healing and for her to regain strength.

He liked to be there in the early evenings when she was alone.

Caer was usually still awake. Tired of giving the impression that she was doing splendidly and she often let her guard down. He had become her confidant

Gillian was there sometimes and they made him feel like family. His family had never had the sort of closeness that Angus saw between the dancers. There were exceptions, like John, Caer's father. He just wasn't father material. Sort of like Angus' own father. He was obsessed with his own work and nothing else mattered. But most of Caer's friends treated her like family. As did Gillian. And they treated him that way too.

A few of them had made overtures of sexual interest at first, but when it became clear he wasn't interested they backed away into friendship. He couldn't remember the last time he had a friend. Someone who liked him for him, not because his father was rich and powerful. Someone of whose intentions he felt sure of. He'd spent most of his childhood and adulthood alone, yet surrounded by people.

Angus turned towards the hospital and began walking, despite his horrible allergies. None of his current meds worked.

Nearly everyone he knew had allergies due to the overwhelming amounts of pollen. Thanks once again to global warming. The wind continued to pick up and the clouds in the sky darkened. Moisture filled the air. It would rain again. Soon.

He found that he quite liked walking the city. He'd never done so in his old life. There was always a car to take him somewhere and he'd never had the time.

He enjoyed being out in the elements. And walking past people's homes, stopping to pet the cats or dogs who came to meet him. He'd never had a pet.

Tonight a brown tabby whirled around his legs, mewing. He petted it and the cat purred and tried to lure him up a sidewalk. Clearly wanting to be let inside.

He laughed and kept walking.

How many people had real lives, real relationships with other people? He'd missed so much in his life, always striving to be a better businessman. To impress his unpleasable father. And without having Core Growth anymore, who was he?

Lost. Still lost.

He needed to change that. He needed to dream his own big dream. To change his life just as Caer was changing hers.

What would that look like?

He hadn't a clue.

Yet.

CHAPTER 16 - CAER

CAER PACED AROUND HER HOSPITAL ROOM FOR THE LAST FEW TIMES. Angus would be here soon. He was bringing one of the Company's vans to pick her up, since she couldn't sit in a car with her wing still bound.

She was finally getting out of this stifling place.

She sipped some indistinguishable juice that had been served with her lunch. Could have been peach. Or apricot. Or mango. Or a mix. She sniffed it, but that was no clue. It just smelled fruity.

Caer stuffed the last of her belongings, her slippers, into her bag and zipped it. The bag bulged. But everything fit.

Her last surgery was five days ago. Now it was all physical therapy. Years of it, according to Dr. Cosby. The doctor was sending a Physical Therapist over from London to get her started and to teach the Company's PT what Caer would need to do in order to heal.

Caer would do whatever it took. In two weeks, if everything healed well, she'd be able to take off the wing binding and at least move her wing.

She could hardly wait.

But for now, she felt relieved to be leaving this place. She hated the too clean smell. She hated the interruptions and noise which happened all night long. Someone coming in to check her blood pressure. To check the pain meds. To take her vitals at 6AM! She hadn't slept a full night's sleep since she got here.

And there were the nightmares.

Falling. Always falling.

She shuddered.

The air in the hospital never smelled fresh. She wanted to breathe fresh air again. She wanted to be in a sweaty, smelly performance hall again. She wanted to be in her own apartment again. She wanted to go home.

But what would it mean to go home? She wasn't a dancer anymore. Maybe she never would be again. She'd need to find a place in the world. She wasn't sure she'd fit in with the Company anywhere. Caer hadn't ever done anything except dance, she had no skills.

Gillian had become a costumer when she got too old to dance well. Other people moved into lighting design or building and painting sets. Other dancers went on to help with running the performances in various capacities. Others worked in advertising, public relations and the business side of the Company.

None of these interested Caer. She just wanted to dance. To fly again. Maybe someone would choreograph a ballet about old decrepit flyers. If she could fly, she'd be in it.

She caught a movement out of the corner of her eye and turned to see Angus.

"Good afternoon," he said.

"Hello."

"How are you doing?"

"I'm so ready to get out of here, I could scream."

"Okay. Then, I'll take a trip down with some of your stuff."

"I got everything together last night. I was so excited to go home."

He picked up most of the bags of gifts she'd received over her three week stay.

Had it really been only three weeks ago that she'd been shot and her world transformed?

Three surgeries in three weeks. She shook her head in an attempt to brush away the memory of a month mostly spent being dazed by pain meds. The entire month had been a mess of pain and nightmares.

She didn't want to relive any of that. Ever again. She hated the way the pain meds made her feel. Totally out of control. As a dancer she was used to controlling every part of her body. When she couldn't, that's when she screwed things up.

Dr. Cosby had told her to just surrender to the meds and to let her body heal. Caer tried, but she couldn't. Not really. Not when she was awake.

Angus came back and picked up the rest of her things and said, "Shall we go?"

She nodded and walked out of the room.

The air in the parking garage wasn't much fresher than that of the hospital, but it felt cooler. She climbed into the back of the large van. It was meant for hauling scenery, props and equipment, so there wasn't seating, except for the wheel wells. Which was good, because until her wing could be free, she wouldn't be able to sit in a car.

Caer grabbed onto a metal hoop on the wall as Angus closed the back door. The van smelled of casein paint, which the Company used to paint sets. It smelled like a performance. If she closed her eyes she'd be able to imagine herself flying.

She didn't. Enough fantasizing. She'd filled up on that in the hospital. She needed a real life. Dreaming wasn't enough.

Angus drove. The van didn't have the capability to be self driven. It was that old.

"I haven't driven in a while, so hang on," he said.

"I don't even know how."

"My father made me learn. Just in case there was some vast technological failure or machine uprising, I think. He's old enough that he never really trusts machines."

She watched the city whiz past the large front window. It was rainy and foggy. Everything was damp and an earthy smell filtered in the cracks where the back door didn't quite meet the floor of the van anymore.

She took deep breaths, trying to suck in the smells of rain and earth.

They finally pulled into one of the Company's garages.

Gillian and Trina were waiting for her at the elevator. Angus stopped the van and got out to open the back door. Gillian hugged her, then Trina did, and they took all the packages from Angus. He closed the back door and waved at them.

"You're not coming up?" Caer asked.

"I've got to park the van back in the scene shop's garage. Then I'll be there."

She nodded and watched him get in and drive off.

The man was a complete mystery to her. A chameleon.

She got in the elevator with Gillian and Trina, feeling the door close behind her, blowing her feathers. The elevator lurched and moved upwards.

"I'm so glad you're finally home," said Gillian.

"Me too," said Trina. "I've missed you at meals so much."

"I'm happy to be home. But it feels weird."

"Why?" asked Trina.

"I don't have a rehearsal to go to. Or class."

"That would be weird. We'll have to find something you can do," said Trina.

The elevator stopped and the door opened. Caer followed them down the hall, around a corner and down another hall to her apartment.

She said, "I don't have my keys. They're in my purse, which the Stage Manager had locked up during the performance."

"And which she gave to me," said Gillian, pulling the keys out of her pocket and jingling them.

"Your purse is in your apartment."

Gillian unlocked the door and walked in, turning on the lights and setting down Caer's bags. Caer walked inside, followed by Trina.

Home, it smelled like home. Patchouli and whatever other familiar scents combined to make it hers. She took a deep breath and relaxed her shoulders which she hadn't realized were tense.

"Surprise!" The sound filled the room and people crawled out from under and behind furniture, walked out of bedroom and bathroom doors, came from behind curtains and her antique screen. Soon there was standing room only.

"Oh my god. How many of there are you and how did you all fit into my apartment?" She laughed.

"It wasn't easy," said Johanna.

A cork popped and champagne was poured into glasses.

"To Caer, may her wing heal and the wind lift her," said Maxine.

"To Caer," everyone toasted.

She sipped the champagne, its fizziness tickling her nose.

And imagined herself flying over a golden field of grass.

Home.

She was home.

CHAPTER 17 - ANGUS

Angus paced inside his nearly empty apartment. The Manager of the Dancers' Complex, Susan, had found this empty apartment for him. He felt relieved to have his own space again. It had been awkward staying at Gillian's. She had so many friends coming and going, he always felt as if he was on show.

His place was furnished with hand me downs from Company members. An old saggy bed with a bulky wooden headboard from one person, a stuffed maroon chair from another, a battered wooden table and chairs from still a different member. They'd found dishes, bedding and lamps for him. Caer had given him a cedar scented candle. Someone else gave him an espresso machine so he could make his own coffee in the mornings.

It made the apartment feel very homey, even if it wasn't exactly his style. The furniture had all been gifts from strangers.

Gifts for which he was extraordinarily grateful. Everyone here was so generous.

Now, he needed to contribute to the Company. He'd chosen to work with the Public Relations Department. He was normally pretty good at that sort of thing.

And he couldn't spend all his time following Caer around.

She needed some space. She'd become dependent on him and she really needed to grow stronger. On her own.

He looked out his window, into the mist, and could even see his two buildings. At times they seemed to almost glow with life. Shimmer. How was it that they'd been able to accomplish this miraculous thing? They'd made an evolutionary leap that was beyond surprising. Difficult to believe it was an accident.

Someone must have contaminated or changed the original growth cells. Or perhaps it had happened after the building was far along. But who? And with what? He wished he had the records, then he could check and see when things started to go askew. It probably wasn't noticeable at the time. But in hindsight...

Had Jonas masterminded that? Or his father? If one or both of them planned to take Core Growth from him, then they would be behind it all. And they would eventually pay. He may not be a brilliant businessman, however, he was tenacious.

But what had they used? Had they known the building would take the change and run with it like this?

No.

He didn't think this part was planned.

But they were certainly taking advantage of it.

He messaged Otis. Perhaps one of the engineers he was talking to could get the info.

Had Jonas shut down the new projects which had been barely started? Were those growth cells affected as well?

He really wanted to go explore the buildings. To find out what made them do what they were doing. But it wasn't safe now, even if he could get in.

He glanced at the clock. Time to go pay for his apartment.

Somehow, he had to come up with something innovative for their next season. A fundraising campaign that all the experienced and brilliant PR people had missed. He wasn't feeling confidant about that.

His confidence had vanished when his life began to fall apart. He needed to get it back. He needed to take back his life.

No one else was going to do it for him.

He straightened his hair, spraying on some product, like Aria had shown him, and checked his shirt and pants to make sure they were clean.

Angus closed and locked the door behind him, slipping the plastic key into his pocket. He took the stairs down to the ground floor. He wasn't getting enough exercise. He should go work out in the dancers' training room. But it felt intimidating working out with all those incredible athletes.

In the PR Office, he found the front desk empty. He walked towards the back, pausing at the door to the main workroom. He wasn't sure if he should go inside.

It was a big room with a central round table in it, surrounded by chairs. The ceiling was high with windows at the top, letting in a lot of light, reflected off the white walls. A large framed Aerial Ballet Poster hung on each wall. A vase of orange chrysanthemums sat in the center of the table.

It was a comfortable rooming for getting a lot of work done together.

Angus could smell the scent of calm floating through the air. So they used the effect-aroma even here.

Margaux was having a heated discussion with Karyn. She stood across the table, leaning on it, from Karyn who was seated, her arms crossed.

"We really need to do better. I can't ask the dancers to add in more performances and still get the same compensation. We need more money. Prices for everything keep going up, that I realize. But we need to respect our performers and staff. We can't do that by continually asking for more from them without raising their pay," said Margaux.

"We just don't have the money Margaux. Our largest donors have all cut back on their giving."

"Well, find more donors."

"Who? We've tapped out everyone in New Seattle," said Karyn.

"I don't know."

Angus stood in the open doorway and listened. This was his first day here. He had ideas, but didn't know if it was appropriate to interrupt. He didn't understand the Company's culture yet.

Margaux noticed him standing there and asked, "Well? Come in. Contribute."

"Excuse me, I didn't mean to interrupt," said Angus.

"I'm all out of ideas," admitted Karyn.

He sat down at the table.

"I have the benefit of being outside the Company and have a different perspective to offer. I don't know if my ideas will work, that's for you to decide. How far away does your reach of donors spread?"

"Just in New Seattle. Maybe a few miles past."

"Why? There's five major aerial ballet companies in the world. London, San Francisco, Sydney, Beijing and here. You should be able to appeal to the entire northwest region. What are you offering people from Fairbanks, Vancouver, Calgary, Denver, Boise, Portland? You need to be drawing from all those cities and the smaller ones too. Really building your company as a destination, art that people with money must come and see. Just to be up on the current culture. Have you done that?" Angus said.

"No," Karyn admitted. "We've always seen ourselves as small potatoes. Our reach hasn't gone out that far."

"Time to expand your reach," he said.

"We could do that." She started tapping notes on her keyboard.

"That means you might have to perform some classics," said Angus.

"We could do that if it would help," said Margaux. She sat down, her fingers tapping on the table as if she was thinking.

"I think it would," said Angus. "Advertise it as entertainment education. You must be familiar with these classics in order to be part of the right circles, because everyone knows the classics and you should have seen them."

"Will that fly?" said Karyn.

"The Company represents high art. You set the standards of what is art. People who don't have an opinion about art can be malleable. New money doesn't always know about art. Neither does old money for that matter. So take advantage of their flexibility and tell them how important it is to their lives to see art. Tell them what is art, without being snobby. Draw on what art has to offer to a person's life," said Angus. "I can see all this, because I don't make art. I'm outside of the field. Both of you live and breathe art. You can't see what happens if people have no access to art."

"It's true, we have no perspective," said Maxine.

"What are you doing as far as educational outreach?" asked Angus.

"We have our flying school for young kids," said Maxine.

"I mean for normal kids. Not for flyers. How are you reaching out to schools and homeschool programs?"

"We're not," said Karyn. She picked up her bottle of water sipped from it.

"Time to start. Get the kids interested. Do a couple of kids' ballets that aren't as bloody and romantic as your normal fare. Perform some matinees just for school kids."

"More work for the Company," said Maxine.

"Yes, it would be. Charge the private schools more and the public schools less or make it free. Have the performers be your younger flyers. Those with a little less experience, those who aren't in your main performances. It will give them more experience and not overwork the main performers. These performances are for your future. They're an investment, just like your flying school for young kids. This one is for your future audiences. And as a gift to the community, for those who can't afford to pay."

"Oh god, you were born in the 'good karma' generation, weren't you?" asked Maxine.

"Yep. My mom truly believed that. What goes around comes around. I got the message," said Angus.

He wasn't so sure his brother got it. But Jonas would definitely get what was coming to him. Angus would engineer a trap for him that made sure of that.

"Any more ideas?" asked Karyn.

"Not at the moment. I'll work more on it. Why don't you show me your mission statement and business plans and financial records for the last couple of years? I'll see what else I can dredge up in my flabby brain."

"I'll get them for you," said Karyn.

"I do have another question. Do you only have the one performance space? Could you do performances in your rehearsal spaces?"

"We could, but the main dancers are already overworked," said Maxine.

"I want you to consider, is there a way to do two performances each night? Maybe do a big classical ballet in the main stage and do something smaller, more alternative, with fewer dancers, in the rehearsal space. Something edgy and new, that would appeal to a completely different audience. Maximize the use of your space and your dancers and perhaps build a larger audience base and increase your income."

"I'll think about that," said Maxine. "I'd have to sit down with lists of dancers, see if it's possible. It's certainly an exciting idea. And there are dancers who hate the classics. They'd thrive with that challenge." She glanced at the clock on the wall and said, "I've got to run. I need to meet with Trudy about our next ballet. I'll check back later today and see if you've come up with anything else."

"We should get all this together and schedule a management meeting," said Karyn.

"Yes," said Maxine as she went through the doorway. "Those are some exciting ideas."

Karyn turned to Angus and said, "Thank you. I think you've just singlehandedly turned the Company around."

"Or, I've just made everyone's lives incredibly complicated."

"I'll find you a screen to work on."

He followed her to another room. This office was smaller, but just as light and airy feeling. Jamie and Max sat at screens working. They waved when Karyn introduced them.

Karyn sat at a screen on a small table and opened several documents.

"This is what we've got. Our business plan is sort of improvisational and scattered. I'm sure you can help focus it for us. And here's our financials. Jamie's in charge of keeping us afloat and she's a genius at it. If you can't figure out something there, she's the one to ask. I'll leave you to it. I've got a PR plan to revise." She got up and left the room.

Angus sat down and began scanning their records. He was looking forward to this. He'd been going nuts without something to sink his teeth into. Losing his company had been both heartbreaking and insanity inducing. He needed to have work, important work, to do. This was perfect.

He relaxed and lost himself in the search for how to help the Company run better.

CHAPTER 18 - CAER

CAER WALKED ON THE INSIDE OF THE LEVEL ONE TRACK IN THE large gym. The cool room smelled of sweat from all the dancers who'd already run this morning.

The big windowless room had three tracks and like all rehearsal and workout spaces, walls covered with mirrors. The track on level two hugged the wall a third of the way up. Level three sat two thirds of the way up the outside wall. Each track was about twenty feet wide. The center of the room had a tall ceiling for flying, making it seem spacious despite the many bodies which could crowd in.

Off to one end of the gym was a large room with weights, mats and other equipment. It was currently filled with a group of giggling ten year olds, learning how to use the weights.

She stopped at one end and took a sip from the purified water fountain. The water was cold and tasted clean. Normal. Not like the awful hospital water, filled with too many cleaning and sterilizing chemicals.

Caer stood up straight again. Funny how such a thing as bending over to get a drink made her feel the pulling in her shoulder.

Taking deep breaths, she tried to do her visualization exercises, letting the muscles loosen and relax back into place. They weren't used to being there. It didn't feel right anymore, but she could tell from the mirrors that it was where it should be.

With her damaged wing still pinioned, she felt uneven, awkward. She was used to unfurling her wings just a bit while walking, not holding them tight to her body. So unless she kept the healthy one tight against her body, muscles always tensed, she was off balance. She'd just have to get used to it.

Caer had been home a week and walking was all the physical activity she was allowed. She couldn't run, it would stress her shoulder joint, Harvey, the Physical Therapist told her.

He'd arrived early, from London. Checked in with her, then flew down to San Francisco. But not before he'd threatened her with physical harm unless she did as he said.

"Nothing but walking. Don't put any stress on your upper body. You need to heal from the surgeries or your wing will never be free again. I'll make sure it's permanently pinioned!" the large, muscular man had said, menace in the tone of his voice.

So she was walking.

She'd spent so long in the hospital that even walking was a challenge. She'd waited until the other dancers went to rehearsals. It was easier having the track to herself. She could mope around and no one would bother her. And she didn't have to deal with the pitying looks everyone gave her.

Caer tried to be positive. She'd spent all week trying to come up with a new dream of who to be. One of the gifts from her friends had been an old fashioned journal. Made of hemp paper. And a real pen. Angus made her write list after list of anything she could think of that she'd like to do. Day after day.

Her hand had blisters. She hadn't written so much in her entire life.

She'd wanted to kill him after the second day. He made her keep doing it.

"You need to have hundreds of ideas about everything you could possibly want to do with your life. Then you'll have three or four really good ones that you really like to choose from."

She'd spent last night looking over the lists till her mind felt blurred. None of the ideas looked interesting or possible.

She just wanted to dance. To heal her wing and dance again. To prove Dr. Cosby wrong.

To prove them all wrong.

She understood the concept that she needed something to occupy her time while she could do nothing physical. Otherwise she'd go crazy. And she also knew it would be a bad idea to overwork her muscles too early. That would inhibit the healing. And until she was healed, she couldn't fly or dance.

So she'd gone along with Angus. She'd explore some of these things. But they weren't a life. She wasn't going to give up on dancing. Not even as she got older. She'd watched too many dancers do that.

Like Gillian. She'd quit dancing when she was pregnant with Caer. She'd opted out of the dance for motherhood. And she'd always claimed to be happy with that choice. But it couldn't be Caer's choice.

John was still dancing and he was Mom's age. He wasn't great, but he still did it. He was the oldest one in the company. There were a couple of other older dancers, Jima and Cass. They didn't get many parts these days, but they still took class everyday and auditioned for every production. Sometimes they got cast. Sometimes not. But they tried and they worked.

Caer had been walking for two hours. She decided to do one more hour and then go find lunch. Then in the afternoon she'd pass the time by watching recorded performances of the London Ballet. New ones were up and available to watch. One of their principals, Anita McIntosh, was one of the most amazing flyers Caer had ever seen. She loved watching her and studied her every movement.

She rounded the track again. One more week. One more week and hopefully, she'd get her wing free.

Then she could begin moving forward again.

CHAPTER 19 - ANGUS

ANGUS LEFT THE DANCER'S COMPLEX AND WALKED BRISKLY TO THE bus stop. The wind was strong, but warmer than a month ago. Spring might actually come this year after all. At least it wasn't raining. But he pulled the jacket close around his neck anyway.

Pollen was heavy in the air today. There had been a danger alert on the news this morning. Global warming hadn't been reversed yet, but they were getting closer to that mark. It would be a long time after that before the excessive pollen amounts would decrease a bit.

He'd taken his meds but they weren't helping much. His eyes itched and were watering. And he felt like tearing them out of his head. He ignored the feeling.

The woman standing next to him was sneezing her head off.

The bus drove up. He got on and sat in a seat alone.

The bus drove away from downtown, topped the hill and went down to Madrona. It passed over the new bridge which spanned what used to be Lake Washington, but was now salt water. Washington Sound.

The Eastside used to contain a fairly large downtown business section. The bridge passed over that area now. It was mainly underwater, although there were no floater here, pulling down the scrap. It had all been taken years ago and repurposed into the bridge.

The area had also been filled with expensive homes, a few of which still stood above water. Most of the wealthy had moved farther East. To higher ground.

Once he was in the new Kirkland business district, he got off. The retail section was jammed with restaurants and pubs. He glanced at the map on his phone and walked until he found the Red-Eyed Crow. He went inside and sat at a table in the corner. The bar smelled of scented candles just being lit by one of the staff, who wore a short black skirt and skimpy white blouse. The bartender, who was completely shaved, down to his nonexistent eyebrows, wore a white muscle shirt and shorts.

It was one of those retro 2050 places. Before the big one and before the flooding. Wood tables and chairs. Bamboo flooring The walls were painted a deep green. Lots of live plants growing under the full spectrum lights. It felt earthy and comforting. And being retro 2050 meant it was echoing the 1980's. Everything looped around.

A saxophone brightly trilled over the sound system in a jazzy song. The bar was about half full. Mostly middle aged men. Lonely men. There were three couples and a table of women too. The women were dressed as if they were looking for men. Skin tight and low cut clothes. He could smell their perfume half way across the room.

Glancing at the menu on the table, he punched in an order for an Irish coffee and lay the payment card Gillian got for him on the scanner. His fingers felt frozen. Holding a coffee would warm them up. The whiskey would help with whatever news Otis had for him. He'd said it was big. Which was why he wanted to meet in person. He had data that he didn't trust sending over the net.

An auto tray brought his drink and he sipped it. The whipped cream was real, or at least tasted like it was. Otis had said this was a good place and he was right. The coffee tasted strong and rich and the whiskey full bodied.

The air was well filtered and his allergies eased somewhat. At least he stopped wanting to tear his eyes out.

The music blared. He recognized all the songs, which meant the music was a decade old. Ever since he'd begun working for his father, Angus had lost track of music. Stopped searching out new artists. There just hadn't been time to live a well rounded life.

The door opened and in walked a large black man. Most people these days were light brown, the mixing of ethnicities. This guy was black as ebony. Tall and wide and bald. Wrapped in a gray raincoat.

He smiled at Angus. It must be Otis. Angus had never seen him before. Otis had probably seen photos of the old Angus, but not since he'd changed his appearance. Angus wore a green shirt so Otis would recognize him.

He sat down across from Angus and struggled with his raincoat for a few minutes before getting it off.

"I kept expecting it to rain today, but it never did. But it's cold out there."

He held out his hand.

"Nice to finally meet you, Alan," he said in his deep, resonant voice, the sound of which put Angus immediately at ease.

"Nice to meet you, Otis."

They shook hands and then Otis ordered.

Angus watched him enter his order. The big man moved slowly and deliberately. Not a wasted motion. As if everything he did was well thought out.

"What do you think of this place?" Otis asked.

"They make a good Irish Coffee."

"I haven't found anything they don't make well. And it's cozy, but discreet. People don't seem to bother me here."

"People bother you?" Angus asked, raising his eyebrows in disbelief.

"Not usually. My size is a deterrent, but there's always some jerk... I try not to encourage them. I don't want trouble."

Angus nodded.

"Nice job on camouflage by the way. I wouldn't have recognized you without the green shirt. And I was looking for you."

"Thanks, it's still an adjustment. The dancers have made me completely change my gestures, my speech patterns, my facial expressions. All those little things that make people recognizable. They're still working on my body shape."

"Talented folks. Give them my contact info. Sometimes I come across people who want to disappear. If they're looking for extra work..."

"I'll do that."

Otis shifted his bulky frame on the small chair.

His drink arrived on the auto tray. It looked like a Manhattan. Otis took it and the tray floated to the ceiling and zipped back to the bar.

He sipped it and a huge smile broke across his face.

Angus was pegging Otis as a gentle giant type. Still, he wouldn't want to mess with him. He was betting Otis wasn't that transparent.

"So, I've been doing more research. I talked to my tech guy and he was able to hack into Jonas' system."

Angus' mouth dropped open. Otis' tech guy must be truly brilliant. Father's companies all used the same security system. It was supposed to be impregnable. Angus knew that was theory, nothing was completely solid, but theirs was the best available.

Angus said, "I didn't think that was possible."

"It is. Apparently my guy used to work for your dad. He helped install the security system. It's been altered somewhat since then, but he managed."

"And?"

"I've got a cube here of what he downloaded," said Otis, pulling a dice sized clear cube out of his pocket and setting it on the table.

Angus took a sip of his drink, pulled out his phone and palmed the cube, touched it to the phone which absorbed it, then slid the phone into his pants pocket.

"What's on it?" asked Angus.

"Enough damning evidence to get your brother locked up for the rest of his life. He's selling everyone out that he can and not covering his tracks quite fast enough."

Angus leaned back in his chair and sipped the coffee, the tastes of sweet and creamy sliding over his tongue, followed up the the smooth slap of the whiskey.

What else had Jonas been up to?

"And there's something else in there," said Otis. "I don't understand the scientific jargon. Maybe you will. But he had an engineer, long gone and I haven't found him yet, put something in the original cells for the building. He expected the contaminant to kill the building. Obviously that didn't happen. You want me to keep looking for the engineer."

"Yeah. I'll need a witness if I want to prove any of this."

"Okay, I'll keep searching. Have you figured out where you're going with all this?" asked Otis.

"What do you mean?"

"Clearing your name? Revenge? You know."

"Not yet. Maybe both. I can't live as a fugitive. Not if I want to stay in this area. My future's up in the air right now. Why do you ask?"

"Just trying to refine my search for information," said Otis. "To see if I can make any sense out of what's going on. There are things that don't fit."

"Like what?" asked Angus.

"Why would your brother try to destroy a major project for a company he's trying to take over? And was he trying to kill you or your father or just frame you?"

"I have more questions. Was my father involved in this takeover plot? What about the attempt on my life? I'm still thinking I was the intended victim. And what exactly is going on with the building?"

"Yeah. I've got any number of possible scenarios. All of which are quite different. That cube I gave you only serves up more questions," said Otis. "Jonas and that engineer, Jonathon the one who shot you, had something else going on."

"I'll look at it and see if I can figure it out."

"Good," said Otis, draining his glass. "Well, I've got work to do, so I'll be in touch. Let me know if you have other questions."

Angus nodded and Otis rose from the chair and left the bar.

Angus lingered for a few minutes thinking about what Otis said about more questions. His life felt filled with questions at the moment. There was little certainty and no firm ground. He finished his drink and stood, sliding into his coat.

Outside the fresh scent of rain filled the air. It drummed down on the pavement and awnings and roofs of buildings, creating a deafening sound.

Lightening flashed across the dark slate sky, followed by a deep rumble of thunder. All the lights went out and plunged the area into darkness. On the other side of the shopping complex lay the road, still lit by headlights.

Angus froze. There wasn't enough light to see by. He dug into his pant's pocket, pulling out his phone and turned on the flashlight. At least he'd be able to see to get to the bus stop. Two men stood near him, one flashed a flashlight into his face, blinding him temporarily.

"Hey," he yelled.

"Freeze, Police," yelled one of them.

He briefly thought about running, but before he could move, one of the men had grabbed him from behind, pulled his hands back and put handcuffs on. His phone dropped to the ground flashlight side up.

The other cop picked it up, clicked it off and put it in a plastic bag.

"Angus Speares, you have the right to remain silent. Anything you say can and will be used against you in a court of law. You have the right to talk to a lawyer and have him present with you while you are being questioned. If you cannot afford a lawyer, one will be appointed to represent you before any questioning if you wish. You can decide at any time to exercise these rights and not answer any questions or make any statements. Do you understand each of these rights I've explained to you? Having each of these rights in mind do you wish to talk to us now."

"I understand. I wish to speak to a lawyer first," he said, with more calm than he felt

"Okay, we'll take you to the station. After you've been processed, we'll let you call your lawyer," the cop said.

The lights flashed on around them and the officer, holstered his flashlight.

A police car floated down from above and he was helped into the back seat. It was awkward trying to climb in with his hands cuffed behind his back. Sitting in the hard plastic seat wasn't so comfortable either.

Angus was trying to concentrate on small details. The large ones threatened to swallow him up. Only one thing was clear.

He must get into his phone and see what that cube contained.

The car took off, rising above the shopping center. He watched as the surrounding area lit up. The lightening must have knocked out the power. A nearby hospital was already lit, they would have had a backup power source. The whole Kirkland district lay in darkness. That would have taken a direct hit of lightening direct to the substation, he thought.

The cops were listening to radio chatter and the one not driving scanned a computer screen and typed on a keyboard.

How had they found him?

Had Otis tipped them off?

If he had, then could Angus trust anything that was on the cube?

The bus had cameras, so did the bar. Had his disguise failed him?

He sat back as comfortably as he could, closed his eyes and tried to replicate the breathing technique Gillian taught him. Tried to clear his mind. Tried to let the panic flow away.

It didn't.

CHAPTER 20 - CAER

Caer stretched, releasing her breath and held the movement, before straightening again. Her entire right side felt limp and weak.

She looked in the mirrors of the empty practice room. Her weak arm, shoulder and wing were hopeless. They all drooped badly.

She was only stretching out and sweat already rolled down her face. She was so out of shape. Never in her entire life had she been this out of shape.

Her mouth was dry. But she wasn't going to stop, even for a drink of water. Not until she'd at least done something.

She'd grown far too soft.

She went to the panel and adjusted the atomizers for hope. The coconutty scent of gorse was immediately apparent.

This might take a little extra help.

She let her feelings flow for once. Didn't try to stuff them back down.

She understood now what Dr. Cosby had been talking about before the operations.

The severing of her muscles had screwed everything up. She

didn't even have enough strength to hold her arm out in front of her for twenty seconds. Cosby had been right. She probably wouldn't fly again.

She wanted to cry.

But she wouldn't. Couldn't.

Couldn't give up.

Physical therapy yesterday had been hell. Harvey unbound her wing and made her try to use it. She couldn't even raise it.

Even babies could raise their wings.

The whole hour had been filled with pain. Emotional and physical. She'd been relieved when it was over.

But with her wing unbound she felt fragile. Like any movement would break it. She still slept on her left side last night, not daring to sleep on her back or even try the right.

She was a coward.

She'd never been a coward before.

And she needed to talk to Angus. And he hadn't come back last night. No one had seen him or knew where he'd gone.

Her belly felt twisted with worry.

She'd become so attached to him. He'd spent the last few months with her, entertaining her in the hospital. Challenging her to widen her view of the world. He made her feel special. And he hadn't pushed her into a romantic liaison, even though she knew he was attracted to her. No, it was beyond attraction. But she knew that he understood what a precarious place she was in her life and was giving her space to recover.

And now he'd vanished.

Even Gillian didn't know where he was. Or Karyn. He hadn't shown up for work today. And Karyn said they'd planned today's meeting two days ago.

Something must have happened to him.

She felt whiny, because she was more worried about herself than him. But she had to deal with herself first. Move through all this. At the moment there was nothing she could do to find him. It wasn't like she could call the police.

Caer breathed and moved into the next stretch that Harvey had given her.

The Company's next season had been posted this morning. The audition dates set.

Caer had tried to ignore it, but she'd found herself opening the message and looking longingly at it.

They were doing La Sylphide. Caer had always wanted to play Slyphide. Since she'd been ten. But the company had never done it before and she'd been too young. Now she was the perfect age. She would have been wonderful as the beautiful, magical spirit.

If she could fly.

She sighed and leaned into the stretch, breathing through the pain.

An hour later she was drenched from the exertion. She went back to her apartment and showered off the sweat. She pulled on a pair of stretchy pants, a blue wrap top and sandals. It was what she used to wear all the time. When her body was in shape and revved up. Now, she felt a little chilled.

She ignored it and walked down to the cafeteria for lunch.

Caer carried the tray with her left arm, her right felt limp and sat down at the same table as Trina and Sophia. The conversation stopped when she showed up.

"Please," she said, "keep talking about the new season. I need to learn to deal with it."

"Okay," said Trina. "I'm so excited that they're doing La Bayadere. I so, so, so, want to dance Nikiya. Who doesn't love a temple dancer?"

"I'm excited about Giselle," said Sophia. "I don't have a chance at a lead, but oh the corps are so wonderful in that ballet."

Caer sipped the curry vegetable soup. It was spicy hot, just the way she loved it. The aromatic heat lit up her mouth and spread through her entire body. She listened to her friends and felt pleased for them and at the same time, sorry for herself.

Karyn walked by with an empty tray.

She leaned over and said, "After lunch can you come see me?"

Caer looked at her. Why did Karyn want to see her?

"Sure."

"I'll be in my office."

Caer watched Karyn put her tray in the dirty dishes bin and left the room.

She ate the rest of her lunch, puzzled by Karyn's request. Did she have to take a job with the Company now that she couldn't fly?

She listened to the chatter of her friends. They tried to include her, but she couldn't concentrate.

"Are you okay?" asked Trina.

"I'm really, really tired. I am so out of shape, it's truly pathetic."

"You'll get better."

"I know. But it's going to be a long haul."

"You can do it. I don't say that lightly. You're the most determined, disciplined and strongest dancer I've ever seen. If anyone can do it, you can."

"We'll see," said Caer.

Could she? Her heart said yes, her body, no.

"I've got to get going. I'll meet you for dinner," said Caer.

"I'll be here. You know me, I don't miss a meal," said Trina.

Caer dumped her tray with the dirty dishes and left the room. She walked as fast as she could to Karyn's office, through corridors, around people and down stairs.

She was breathing heavily by the time she got there and stopped outside the office to catch her breath. She needed another shower, but it had felt good to move so quickly. Her whole right side ached. When she got back to her apartment, she'd take another painkiller.

Caer opened the glass door into the administration offices. Karyn sat at the main desk, looking at a screen.

"Oh hi, have you seen the news?"

"No," said Caer. "I never watch the news."

"You might want to see this," said Karyn, flipping the screen so it projected onto the wall and turning up the volume.

"No word yet on whether Angus Speares is going to plead guilty. His lawyer said there will be no comment for the time being. There's also no word on where he's been hiding for the past few months since he disappeared," said the woman, wearing the KIRO tattoo on her cheek.

Behind her flashed Angus' picture. So he'd been arrested. Caer's heart sank. She needed to go see him.

"Did he turn himself in? Do you know where he's at?"

"No, they caught him. He's in jail, somewhere," said Karyn.

"Can you find out where?" asked Caer.

"You gonna go see him?" asked Karyn.

"Yeah. I think he could probably use a friendly face."

"I'll try to find out," said Karyn. "But they might not let you see him."

"Why?" asked Caer.

"Because he's suspected of hiring the guy who shot you. Mistakenly shot you, of course, but shot you just the same. You'll be a witness in the trial."

"I'll refuse."

"I don't think you can," said Karyn.

"Crap."

"And even if you could, it's a fact that you were shot. It's not like you can deny it."

Karyn typed on her keyboard and shuffled through several screens. "He's in Central Holding. It's in the Northlake area. You want me to come with you?"

"Would you?" asked Caer.

"Sure. I'd love to see him. I want him back. So far he's almost singlehandedly helped us turn the direction of the Company around. He's brilliant. I'll order a car for us."

"I'll run up and change. What garage shall I meet you in?"

Karyn flipped to a different page and typed a bit.

"1:00 in the Debussy Garage."

"Okay."

Twenty minutes later Caer stood in the garage. It was chilly out still. Spring hadn't really begun. She wished for a coat instead of the wrap sweater which didn't make her warm enough.

Karyn pulled up, sitting in the back of a white car. Caer slid into the back and sat in a dancer's seat, made specially for flyers. It had a narrow back which fitted between her wings and seat belts placed to fasten across the body, but not the wings.

When Caer was strapped in, Karyn said, "Go."

The car moved slowly through the garage and out into the pouring rain. There'd be no view today. The humidity in the air huddled around the car, making her feel safe. The car slid through the gray blanket of rain towards their destination.

Karyn had curtained the windows making them opaque. Caer always wondered why people did that, but many in the Company did. They tried to shelter the flyers from the outside world and peering eyes, as if that would make them feel more a part of the world, not like the strange, exotic creatures they all were.

Half an hour later, the car pulled up in front of the Central Holding Building. It was an imposingly tall place, fifty or more stories high and totally black. The only windows were in the front entrance. She shivered and got out of the car and walked through the pouring rain.

Her wings were drenched by the time she entered the revolving door. Karyn followed her and Caer watched the car drive off to park itself.

Why had she come? Would he even want to see her?

The door was a tight fit, she knew it was meant to be. Its purpose was to make you feel trapped and helpless. Knowing that didn't make the feeling any better. She hated having her wings pinned to her sides, worrying the tips would get caught somewhere.

Inside, they passed through several detectors for metal, chemicals and whatever type of plastics they were worried about these days. Then they were funneled to a counter, where the line divided into three and three people waited behind it.

Human people. Not androids or screens. Real humans.

She and Karyn made their way to the front of the line and spoke to a short, chubby dark haired woman.

"We'd like to see Angus Speares, please."

The woman typed something.

"Relatives?" she asked.

"No, just friends."

"I'll need to ask permission from the person in charge. Names please."

They gave their names and waited.

"She says you'll need to talk to her. She's in 3820," said the woman, pointing to a bank of elevators.

They rode alone in the elevator, saying nothing. Caer expected it was monitored. The elevator was lined with smoky colored mirrors and felt as oppressive as the rest of the building.

They made their way up to the 38th. floor and to the office. The decor was all in white. It was almost blinding. Carpet, walls & ceiling, too much white. How did they ever keep it clean?

There was no noise. It was as if the carpet sucked it all up.

It smelled artificial. Chemical. Plastics from the carpet, furniture and paint.

Karyn knocked on the door and opened it. Caer followed her inside. A woman with tightly cropped brown hair and wearing a navy police uniform looked up from her screen. An air purifier hummed from a corner behind the desk. The woman suffered from allergies, as did most people these days.

"I'm Captain Pietus," she said, studying both of them.

"I'm Caer and this is Karyn Salassa. We're here to see Angus Speares."

"And you're not family."

"No, we're friends."

"How do you know Mr. Speares?"

"He stayed with us for a time," said Caer.

"Harboring a fugitive is a crime."

"And just who was the crime against? I was the one who was shot, Captain," said Caer, sneering.

The woman stared at her.

Karyn did too. Caer knew Karyn could tell she was furious. Caer wouldn't be surprised if she saw steam coming out her nose. She was fuming at the Captain's subtle contempt.

Caer knew she was being reassessed.

She stared back at the woman, cooly. As if she was inferior. This woman understood pecking order. She paid this woman's salary. She would not be intimidated.

"Why do you, the victim, want to see your assailant?"

"He didn't pull the trigger and I don't believe he organized it either. And that bullet wasn't meant for me."

"A jury will make that decision. Why do you want to see him?"

"He's my friend. I want to make sure he's okay."

"And what about you?" the Captain asked Karyn.

"He's been working on the Company's fundraising campaign. He's a coworker and a friend as well."

The Captain leaned back in her chair and stared at them.

Finally, she said, "You can each see him for five minutes."

"Thank you," said Karyn and gently took Caer's left arm to usher her out.

"Take the elevator to B12. I'll let them know you're coming," said the Captain.

As they got into the elevator Karyn whispered, "Remember the Rules: # 32 - Do not attack the Choreographer."

Caer sighed. "I'll try not to."

They were silent and the elevator dropped to the basement and beyond.

Down on B12, the elevator opened to blackness. Everything down here was black. The black tiled floor glistened beneath the bright lights. They walked through 5 detectors for things Caer couldn't even guess at. There were officers everywhere. After the detectors, she and Karyn had to go through a pat down search. The officer didn't really know what to make of her wings. Or how to search them.

"Raise your wing higher please."

"I can't."

"You raised your other wing higher."

"Because that one hasn't had a bullet go through it," she said, glaring at her.

"Oh, you're that dancer."

"Yes, I'm that dancer."

She and Karyn were put in a small waiting room after the search. It too, was black. There were chairs, a couch and a small table, but nothing Caer could sit on. She felt too restless anyway and paced around the room, her hard shoes click, clacking on the tile.

She wasn't used to being so disrespected, even though she understood the reasons.

At premieres and fundraisers dancers were fawned upon. She'd been treated as special her entire life, the first human born with wings. At the worst dancers were looked upon as particularly beautiful freaks. Strange creatures who endured huge amounts of pain to fly and to be beautiful.

She'd never spoken to the police before, let alone been searched. She was usually surrounded by security guards when she went out in public. It felt strange to be on the other side.

Finally the door opened and an officer came in and said, "Please come with me."

Caer followed her down the hallway and into a small room. Angus was sitting on the other side of a glass wall. She perched on the front edge of a straight chair in front of the glass, adjusting her wing tips.

"Angus, how are you?"

"Caer. You shouldn't have come," he said.

He looked pale, but not cool pale, unhealthy pale. There were dark circles under his eyes from allergies and she guessed this section didn't get air purifiers like Captain Pietus' office. Pollen got in everywhere.

"How could I not come? You helped me when I needed you. Now it's time for me to help you."

"Nothing you can do," he said, his smile looked weak.

He reminded her of a dancer who'd given up. She'd seen them. Kids like her who couldn't take the long hours of building up their bodies. The long rehearsals, the strengthening of their muscles and their mental discipline. Kids who didn't want to dance badly enough to overcome everything else.

"There must be something," she said. She was not going to let him give up.

"All the proof I had was on my phone. My phone's dead though. So my lawyer said." He shrugged.

"Do you trust your lawyer?" she asked.

"I don't know. I've never used him before. I couldn't exactly use our normal family's firm. Jonas and my father are using them."

"I'll see if I can find you a better one," she said. "What else?"

"My lawyer said he can't get hold of a friend. Otis Jackson. I really need to talk to him."

"Okay, I'll make sure it happens."

"How are you?" he asked.

"I'm good. Other than being cranky, bored and hating physical therapy. It's going to be a long road back. But I'm coming back," she said, clenching her jaw.

It occurred to her that she was only saying that to help him feel strong. But then Caer realized that as she said it, she believed it.

"Good for you. I'm glad you're still determined. You are still trying to find something to occupy your down time though, aren't you?"

"I've found something," she said. "Apparently, I need to get you out of jail.

"Time's up," said the officer.

"I've got to go," she said. "You take care of yourself. I'll be back as soon as I've done both those things."

"I've missed you so much," he said.

Before she left the room, she turned back.

The look on his face was heartbreaking.

And she realized how much she loved him.

CHAPTER 21 - ANGUS

ANGUS SAT IN THE PRISONER WAITING ROOM. AT A BLACK TABLE, IN a black room. The glass in front of him was clear, but imbedded with metal.

His heart was sobbing. It wanted more time with Caer. Soon she'd be beyond his reach altogether.

Perhaps she already was.

His lawyer told him he didn't have a snowball's chance in hell to win.

All the time that Angus had been hiding his family's firm of lawyers had been gathering evidence and feeding it to the police. Helping them firm up the case against him. Before he was even caught.

So his lawyer was trying to get him to plead guilty.

Angus refused. He wasn't guilty and he wouldn't lie and say he was.

Karyn walked in the door and sat in front of him.

"Angus, Caer says you've given up."

"I wouldn't put it that way," he said.

"Well, what way would you put it?" Karyn asked, leaning back and staring at him.

She was challenging him.

"I've taken a look at my chances and calculated the odds."

She leaned forward and said, "You will not gamble with that girl's heart, damn you. She's got enough problems without you screwing things up. Now get that sharp mind of yours going and find your way out of this."

"I've been sitting here for two days trying to do just that. Without the information on my phone, without a decent lawyer, I can't think of how to move forward."

"What information on your phone? They should be able to give your phone to the lawyer."

"I dropped it. I've been told it's dead."

"By whom?"

"My lawyer."

"Get a new lawyer."

"Caer's on it already. But if my lawyer's not working for me, which I suspect, then if my phone was working, they've already got the info on it and will use it against me."

"What's on the phone."

"I don't know. I'd just gotten it. Hadn't even had a chance to open the files."

"Where did you get it from?" asked Karyn.

"I don't want to implicate the person," said Angus.

"Well, I'll make sure you get a new lawyer. I'll talk to the Company's lawyers and get a referral for a criminal lawyer. Don't give up. I'll make sure there's someone here to see you tonight, tomorrow by the latest."

"Why would you do this?" he asked.

"Oh so many reasons. One, you've made such a huge difference in the Company's fundraising efforts. I can't tell you how much help you've been. And we've only had time to implement a few of the changes you recommended. Think what would happen if we had you with us for months on end?"

"You'd kick me out," he said.

"Second, Caer needs you. You've done so much for her and she still needs you. She's getting close to the crumble point. I've seen a lot of dancers quit when the physical therapy really gets hard. And she's almost at that point."

"Not much I can do for her. She has to do it."

"But your presence helps strengthen her. You many not see it, but I can and so can Gillian. Caer may or may not realize it. But she needs you all the same. I don't know if she can come back from this or not. But she thinks she can. So you better be there."

"I still don't see why you'd go to the trouble to help me. Guilt by association, that sort of thing. You don't want to taint the Company with that. And I don't see how I can come out of this clean."

"God, how can you be so stupid? The Company takes care of their own. That's how we survive. And you are now one of us. You are going to be acquitted. Get that through your thick skull. And act as if that's the case. Be strong. Be a dancer. Even if you can't fly, you can still carry yourself with dignity. So do it."

"Yes ma'am," he said, sitting up.

She nodded at him.

The officer came into Karyn's side and said, "It's time."

Karyn stood and asked, "Anything else I can do?"

He shook his head.

"Well, till I see you again, work on adjusting your attitude."

She turned and went out the door.

The guard came to get him and returned him to his cell.

An 8 by 8 gray room with a toilet in the corner and a bed on the other side. A dim light on the ceiling. Nothing else. No screen to watch or listen to. Nothing to read. Nothing to do except think about the crime he committed.

Or lack of crime.

He lay back on the cot.

Was his lawyer working for Father and Jonas?

He'd asked the man yesterday.

"How could you even suspect such a thing?" said Anthony DeLauren, with puffed up shoulders and a snarl in his voice. His aftershave made Angus want to gag. It must have been strong for him to be able to smell it through his stuffed up nose.

"I'm asking, because if ever a defense tactic came across my desk like yours, I'd call it giving up."

"I'm not telling you to give up," said DeLauren, obviously backpedaling. "I'm telling you to face reality. You've no proof that anyone told the engineer to fire that shot. The police do. They interviewed the man, who claims you are behind everything. They only way to get out of this without you being put into prison forever, is to plead guilty. I know you've told me that you're not guilty. I'm not saying you are. I'm simply telling you to say that you are. It'll knock years off your sentence."

Angus had laughed so hard he snorted and refused to say anything else to the fool.

Never, in his entire life had a lawyer told him there was only one option.

He'd known he needed a new lawyer, but felt too despondent to do anything about it. Besides the poor air filtration Angus suspected the jail used effect-aroma too. Adding a touch of suffering to hopelessness and a heavy dose of apathy.

He hoped Caer would get in contact with Otis. Otis would figure out that Angus hadn't gotten a chance to see the contents of that cube or had lost the info. He'd know what to do.

At least that would work if Otis hadn't been paid off and turned him in. He still wasn't a hundred percent sure about that.

If Caer or Karyn got him a decent attorney, then the attorney could contact Otis. And perhaps find out how the police found him.

Either way, it was out of his hands for now.

All he could do was hope.

He fell asleep waiting for dinner and dreamt of dancing with Caer.

He was in a tux and she wore a long white, shimmering gown. Her hair glimmered, even her wings had rhinestones on them. They were in a huge candle lit ballroom all alone. Waltzing. Swirling around the room and the feathers of her wings were lifted by the wind their movement created. Caer floated into the air and held onto him.

"Fly," she said. "Fly you can do it."

He was trying and almost left the ground.

The guard woke him up before he could find out what happened next in the dream.

"Dinner," the guard said, sliding the metal plate of food in through a slot in the leaden wall.

Could he have flown?

He might never know now.

Or maybe he could go back into the dream tonight.

That was something to look forward to.

CHAPTER 22 - CAER

Caer gazed out the shaded car windows, listening while Karyn contacted the Company's law firm.

"No, Eric. Your assistant was right. I need the name of the best lawyer you can find who does criminal law."

Karyn continued, "No, it's not a Company member as such. We had a friend helping us with PR and well, just being an all around helpful guy. Now he's being nailed to the wall."

Karyn tapped a number into her phone. And another. And another, obviously adding the numbers of possible criminal lawyers, while continuing her discussion with the Company's law firm.

"Okay. I should tell you, the man is Angus Speares, and his family are the the people prosecuting him. Their lawyers have been instrumental in helping the police. I don't know what firm they use, but we don't want that firm."

Caer pulled out her phone and searched for Otis Jackson. There was only one. A Private Investigator. Why would Angus want her to contact someone like that? She sent the man a message.

"Angus Speares is in trouble. In jail. He asked me to contact you. Can we talk?"

Karyn continued her conversation, "Really? I've heard of her. She's so high profile. Is she really that good?" Karyn paused, then said, "You're right. This is going to be a media circus either way. Okay, if your gut feeling is that strong, then we'll call her first."

There was a long pause as Karyn obviously listened to the person on the phone. The city rolled by, it was dark now and Caer could see the lights flash by even through the curtained windows.

Karyn said, "Thank you so much Eric. You've been so helpful."

She punched in another number.

"Yes, could I please speak to Ms. O'Hara? I'd like to hire her. Yes, I understand that. Eric Markus recommended I call her. He represents us, the Zephyr Ballet Company of New Seattle. One of our employees needs her help. Angus Speares, I'm guessing you've heard of him? I thought so. Please have her give me a call. Thank you." Karyn clicked her phone off, letting out a huff at the same time.

"Bitchy assistants," said Karyn.

"Will she call back?" asked Caer.

"Yes, she's a media vampire. But Eric says she's brilliant. Angus' name will draw her. As will the connection to us."

"I sent a message to Otis Jackson. He's a Private Investigator."

"Interesting. Wonder if he was working on something for Angus."

"I hope so. And I hope he's found something."

They rode in silence for several minutes when Caer's messages pinged.

She glanced at it. Then typed in a reply.

"Fromage, on Ballard Hill, thirty minutes," she told the car.

"Jackson?" asked Karyn.

Caer nodded. She hoped Fromage wasn't too crowded or too vacant. She was glad Karyn was coming with her.

The car pulled up in front of a brightly lit restaurant. It looked trendy, but this was Monday night. Not generally a popular night to eat out.

Caer got out, followed by Karyn and the car drove off to park.

Caer walked into the busy restaurant. It was retro 2060's. The golden age. Before the big one. When Seattle had valleys and the waterfront wasn't filled with the debris of old buildings. The walls were made of faux wood, which made for a warm feeling on this cold, rainy night. Plants hung everywhere, walls and ceiling. The smells from the kitchen made Caer's mouth water, garlic and onions were the first to register.

The android Host looked at them and Caer said, "We're meeting someone. Otis Jackson."

"Oh, Mr. Jackson is already here. I'll take you to his table," said the android. He led them to a table in the back corner. It was close to the bar area and the kitchen. It was a booth.

Caer said, "I'll need a chair, please."

The Host said, "Of course, I'll be right back."

"I'm sorry," said the tall man at the table. "I didn't know you were a flyer. I would have chosen a different table."

"It's fine," she said. "I'm used to it."

Karyn stood until a chair was brought for Caer.

"So you're Caer. And you must be Karyn."

"And you must be Otis Jackson," said Karyn.

"Yes. I'm not sure what Angus wants," he said. "I gave him the cube at our last meeting and then I heard he was arrested."

"He said something about some proof that he needed was on his phone. And his lawyer told him the phone was broken," said Caer.

"Aah. And I saw him put the cube in his phone. So he maybe didn't even see it. Who broke into his phone? The cops or the lawyer."

"He's not sure the lawyer's working for him," said Karyn.

"We're trying to get him a new lawyer," said Caer.

"Who?" asked Otis.

"Willa O'Hara."

Otis whistled.

"Angus is gonna open a big can of worms with her."

"What exactly does that mean?" asked Caer.

"He's going fishing and he's gonna catch some big fish."

"Oh," said Caer, not really understanding.

Karyn asked, "Do you have another copy of the cube?"

"I always make copies. It's in a safe place. Who shall I deliver it to?"

"I'll call you when we have a new lawyer for him," said Karyn.

The waiter came over and handed out menus.

"You ladies should stay for dinner. The food here is fabulous."

"I can't wait," said Caer. "It smells wonderful."

They stayed for dinner and Otis filled their heads with stories of Old Seattle.

CHAPTER 23 - ANGUS

ANGUS WAITED IN THE LAWYER CLIENT ROOM, WEARING THE fuchsia colored jumpsuit and flip flops. His lawyer wasn't there yet.

This room was painted gray, just like everything else down here. Gray and depressing. It consisted of a table and two chairs. Hard, old fashioned chairs. Straight chairs. It was a utilitarian room, filled with despair and hopelessness.

He felt groggy. He'd been spending most of his time sleeping. There wasn't much else to do other than try to figure out how to get evidence against Jonas if Caer failed. His allergies made him sleepy too. He had no meds.

He didn't know if Otis made backups. It was the smart thing to do, but there might be client confidentiality problems if he did and someone else got hold of a backup.

He'd been dreaming of Caer again. And woke up wondering if he had a chance with her. She couldn't have been put in his life for no reason, could she?

Was fate just messing with him?

He rubbed his face, feeling the ever present stubble. He didn't care about shaving. Maybe just before the trial.

The door opened and a guard escorted in a tall, redheaded woman. She looked vaguely familiar, but he couldn't place her.

She glanced at Angus and said to the guard, "Can we get two coffees, please."

"I'll see what we can find."

He went out and she put her screen on the table and leaned over to shake his hand.

"Mr. Speares, I'm Willa O'Hara, your new lawyer. The Zephyr Ballet of New Seattle has hired me to represent you, if you'll have me."

Then her face clicked into place. He'd seen her on many, many newscasts. She represented countless famous defendants in criminal cases. And mostly got them off.

The shock of seeing her here, made him see the reality of what was going on. He was being tried for attempted murder.

The shock woke him up.

"Yes, I certainly will," he said, shaking her hand.

"Good," she said, sitting down. "We've got a lot of work to do."

She tapped on her screen and opened files.

The guard came in with two coffees. Angus picked one up gratefully and sipped from the paper cup. The coffee tasted horrible, burnt, but at least it had some flavor.

"I've seen the news and heard a lot of rumors. I want you to tell my your side of this. From the beginning. Don't leave anything out. Everything you tell me is, of course, confidential."

He told her everything that had happened at the ballet and about the building being out of control, his suspicions that he was being framed for the shooting by Jonas and perhaps his father. That he was the intended victim of Rodriguez. That part of the goal was to get him out of the way so Jonas could take over his company.

"Have you seen this information that Mr. Jackson gave you?"

"No, not yet. I was arrested just after I received it and I dropped my phone. My last lawyer told me it was broken."

"I asked for your phone just before I came down here and was told there was no record of a phone being checked in with the rest of your belongings."

"Then you can assume that my brother or father have the phone and its contents," he said. "I believe the lawyer was working for them, not me."

"Well, you won't have that problem with me, I can assure you. I'm hired by the Ballet to represent you." She shifted in her chair. "I'm guessing that none of this information will surprise you. But you must realize little of it will be admissible in court, because it was stolen by Mr. Jackson. We can try to find other sources for some of it. We can try to get it legally, but if your family knows what we're looking for, they'll have locked things down quickly. Destroyed files, that sort of thing."

She pushed the screen over to him and he skimmed the documents.

There was Jonas' appointment schedule, which included meetings with Rodriguez. Records of site visits to the building, before Caer had been shot and Jonas took over the company. Lab reports of the initial phase of the buildings cell growth. Those were from two years ago. Otis had included phone records from a number registered to Jonas, that Angus didn't recognize. Those records mostly consisted of calls to Rodriguez and went back three years. There was no sign of his father in any of the records, but he may have kept his hands out of it.

Angus leaned back. He'd had no idea Jonas knew Rodriguez, but apparently Jonas had planted him in Angus' business many years ago. He'd been the person most instrumental in all phases of the current building's growth.

Willa said, "The phone records are admissible in court. Some of the other documents are a little dicey."

"I had no idea Rodriguez was planted in Core Growth by Jonas. He must have been the person who added something to the initial growth cells. Which is why the building went crazy. I wonder what he added."

"It looks like Jonas has been planning this for a long time."

"I'd say so. I just don't know if my father is part of it or not."

"If he is, he's kept his hands clean. Would he really sacrifice his son?"

"If he's involved, he's already sacrificed me."

"Good point," she said. "And Mr. Jackson, you trust his confidentiality?"

"Yes, I believe so. Although I was arrested just after I met with him. Could have been coincidence. I rode a bus with cameras. I sat in a bar, also with cameras. Or perhaps Jackson turned me in."

"I'll see what I can find out about your arrest. And I'll tell Mr. Jackson to keep digging. See what he can find in Core Growth's records. See if we can find out exactly what was put into those initial growth cells."

"I think we need to know that," said Angus, "but I don't know if anyone can tell us except Rodriguez."

"Well, we'll see what we can do. I'm going to try to get your initial hearing postponed. Since you've had a change of lawyers, it'll give us a little more time."

He nodded.

"Okay, then, I'm off to set things in motion."

Angus' head was already whirling. This woman was a fireball. Just what he needed to burn past Jonas.

She went out the door and a guard came to get him and take him to his cell. He swallowed the rest of the awful coffee first.

Once again, he wished he had access to a screen. What had Rodriguez added to those cells? He wanted to know what the building was doing and why. Had it been planned? Or had Rodriguez and Jonas simply been trying to destroy the building? Destroy his company at any cost? The questions whirled around and around in his head until it ached.

CHAPTER 24 - CAER

CAER WAS IN A SMALL BRIGHTLY LIT REHEARSAL ROOM. IT SMELLED of the sweat of the five dancers who'd been using it before her. They had been working on a project, hoping to develop it into a performance piece. They were so young, maybe fourteen. She remembered herself back then. Tall, gangly and unsure of herself.

Now she was just tall and unsure of herself. Of her failing body.

Caer chewed mint gum, snapping and popping it as she worked her way through the stretches Harvey had given her. Just to the point below pain.

"If you go too far, if you hurt yourself, it'll be a setback. You'll have to take a week off. That joint is still tender. I know it is, so don't try and tough your way through these exercises. Don't push too hard. I know you're not stupid. I know you're in a hurry, so be conservative and don't do more than your body can handle right now. Pay attention to the pain. It's telling you that you've gone too far and you need to rest and let it heal," he'd said.

She hated him.

She hated all of this.

Caer just wanted to fly again.

Now.

To be free of worrying about what was too much or was she working too hard or not enough.

To be free of worrying about Angus and the mess he was in.

There had been no words of romance or lust or even interest spoken between them.

How could there be? They were always separated by a glass barrier.

But the feelings were there all the same.

She felt it from him and she hoped he was able to pick up her emotions from gestures and her intent.

She visited him every day now. Even if she had nothing to say. She couldn't not go see him.

They were bound together as surely as that bullet meant for him had severed her wing joint and shattered her life.

She'd overcome the injury, but not the connection with him. Every day it strengthened and grew and filled her with joy.

The certainty that she'd overcome her pain and fly and dance again mingled with the certainty that he'd be freed and regain his life again.

Together they'd pursue their separate dreams.

So she stretched and pushed, just enough, to strengthen her wobbly muscles.

And tried to think of a way she could help free him.

She spent one minute slowly moving her damaged wing. It didn't hurt but the muscles were so very weak. She repeated the same with her good wing, for five minutes. It had gotten sloppy and out of shape. She longed for the sheer physical strength of those teenagers.

She dreamt of flying every night. Strangely, she almost always found herself flying out in the open, over a wild, grassy area with the ocean in the distance. She caught the wind and rode it like surfers rode waves.

In the dream, she could smell the salty, kelpy air. Almost feel the spray from the waves on her face. It was even better than flying in a theatre.

Even better than performing.

In the dream sometimes Angus chased her, down below in the grass, laughing. Sometimes he had black wings to match his dark hair. He flew around her, diving in and out. Playing.

Either way the dreams were always magical. She didn't want them to end and have to come back to the reality of pushing towards the pain every day. Of making only minuscule improvements.

And she didn't have any solutions to helping Angus. Other than just showing up every day. To show support. And her love.

And hope that he understood.

CHAPTER 25 - ANGUS

Angus sat in the brightly lit conference room beside his lawyer. These were his lawyer's offices. Decorated in classic cream, speaking of elegance and power. For the public.

He sipped an espresso from a cream colored cup, reveling in the taste of perfect coffee.

He'd cut his hair, no more long bangs covering his face, although the tips of his hair were still dyed and he'd left the tattoo of the dancer on his cheek. The purple dye in his irises had faded over the last week. He'd even put a black suit on.

They were waiting for Jonas' lawyer to show up. The air here was filtered for optimum human performance in contrast to the jail cell he'd been in just hours before.

Unlike the others, he still had an allergy hangover. Obviously, the poor ventilation was part of the prison system weighing against the prisoner. Keeping them off balance.

Certainly not part of the innocent until proven guilty theory. That was so old Seattle.

The last twelve hours had been dizzying. So much had happened, he could barely keep up.

Criminal charges against him had been dropped as Willa

brought new evidence to light which pinpointed the relationship between Rodriguez and Jonas.

Rodriguez must have gotten scared. He confessed that his target had been Angus and he had been working for Jonas. He was still in jail. Angus looked forward to talking to him about the growth cells for the building. That would have to happen later.

Jonas hadn't been arrested. Yet. But Caer had been more than willing to press charges.

Willa had threatened to file charges against Jonas over the illegal takeover of the business. She'd included Father in her threat, since he was in charge of the Board of Directors.

She had told Angus as he was released, "I'm on shaky ground here. I'm not up to date on business law. I turned towards criminal law several years ago, but I can start the proceedings. You'll need to find someone to take over."

"I'm a business lawyer," he said, grinning. "You're doing just fine. I'll tell you if you need to alter your course. This is mainly a threat. I want some leverage to do what I intend. The threat of a highly publicized lawsuit is all I want. If it goes forward, I'll consider your resignation."

"So you want me for the drama?" she asked.

"Yes. Father hates drama. He'll do everything he can to avoid it."

"What about Jonas?"

"Personally, I doubt anyone will ever find him," said Angus. "He'll have fled the country and who knows where to? But I mean to take everything of his that I can get my hands on. It won't ruin him, but it'll hurt."

Jonas' lawyer finally walked in the door. John McCammon. He was Father's lawyer. Old, stodgy and experienced.

Angus stood and offered his hand, "Mr. McCammon."

McCammon held out his hand, "Call me John, please. Hello Angus. Ms. O'Hara, it's a pleasure to meet you. Nasty business this, though."

"You can call me Willa," she said, shaking hands.

"Willa, okay." He sat across from them and opened his screen. Then looked at both of them.

"We've made our initial move," said Willa, "what's your clients' reply?"

"Right down to business, eh? You young people have no time for pleasantries."

Angus said, "I see nothing pleasant about my family trying to murder me and taking away my livelihood."

John nodded, "Your family, it wasn't your entire family. Only Jonas has been implicated by the evidence that was found."

Angus said, "You're right, at this point in time we only have evidence implicating Jonas. I don't believe for a moment that Jonas slipped all this past Father. Father's too sharp for that. The police will keep digging and so will we. And everything we get will be released to the media. Every single thing. If we need, this will be a crime tried by the media. My lawyer is brilliant with the media, perhaps you've noticed. I've nothing left to lose. My family has taken everything away from me and backed me into a corner. I'm quite prepared to go this route."

John nodded, "But you are willing to consider other options? Ones that won't hurt your family?"

"Oh, I think all the options will hurt my family. But yes, I have other options in mind."

"Would you be willing to share them?" asked John.

"I want full control of Core Growth. I want to own the company outright with no strings attached. I'll be creating a new board of directors and I choose who stays and who goes."

John nodded and tapped on his screen.

Angus continued, "I want complete ownership of all of Jonas' companies, properties and shares. With the ability to sell what I want, when I want. No strings attached."

Willa sucked in her breath, almost silently.

John leaned back in his chair. "I don't think that's possible. There are too many complications."

"It's possible. It's complicated, but I'm sure that Father has the ability to iron out those complications," said Angus.

Checkmate.

Willa leaned back in her chair, not shifting her facial expression a bit, but a smile came into her eyes. "I've just sent you the documents to complete the transfers."

John shook his head. "I don't know if your father will agree to this."

"In exchange for all this, I'll leave both Father and Jonas alone, provided they leave me alone. I can't stop the police from hunting Jonas, but I won't press charges. I can't speak for the dancer, or the ballet. He ruined her life and robbed them of a star performer they spent years grooming," Angus shrugged. "There are consequences for our actions."

John said, "I don't think your father will agree to all this."

"Well, that's his choice. As I said, I'm more than happy to let this be tried by the media."

"What do you get out of that? You won't get your company back," asked John.

"I get the satisfaction of seeing justice done. Of Jonas being known for what he is and of my father being shown as behind it all. A man who would kill one of his sons. A man who has no heart. We have a media campaign planned which will sear your eyeballs. It's only a pity that it's all true."

"That's a terrible thing to say."

"I've only just begun," said Angus. "Tell that to my father. He knows me well enough to know how determined I can be."

"Anything else?" asked John.

"We'll need an answer in 24 hours," said Angus.

"Well, I'll give him your message. I wouldn't hold out much hope, if I were you," said John, shaking hands with both of them.

Angus said, "It matters not one bit to me, what he decides. Either way, I win. He's already lost."

Willa just watched, silently.

After the door closed, Willa let out her breath.

"Remind me never to make you an enemy," she said.

"What else can you do to a man who tried to murder you?" he asked her.

"I don't know. But you're fearsome to watch. Why did you give up law?"

"I don't like being like this. I don't like being my father. It's not who I am. But if I have to, I will be. So, if there's no response by the end of the day, you should file the Ballet's lawsuit."

"That soon?"

"It's just a nudge. But it will get his attention."

"What are you going to be doing?"

"I'm going back to jail. I want to talk to Rodriguez. While he's still feeling penitent and before he's unavailable."

"What do you mean unavailable?" asked Willa.

"I have a feeling he's not going to live a long life."

"Who?"

"Jonas. Or perhaps my father. But it won't be traceable. It'll be a scuffle among prisoners. Or with a guard, self defense. Something like that."

"Send me a message when you're done talking to him. I'll report a threat to his life. That might buy him some time."

Angus said, "I'll do that. Not sure it'll do any good though."

CHAPTER 26 - CAER

CAER STOOD AT THE BARRE, STRETCHING HER LEGS. SHE GLANCED AT the mirrors on the wall. Sweat dripped down her sides, wetting the workout clothes and she felt tired. She needed a shower, she'd smell better.

Gregor stood watching her. Peeling an orange of its skin, in one long piece. She could smell it from where she was. It made her mouth water, she was ready for lunch.

"Your wing doesn't droop anymore, have you noticed that?"

She looked back at the mirror and said, "I wasn't sure if I was seeing that or not."

"It's a good sign. The joint's recovering. I think you can move to the next level. If you're ready."

"If you say I'm ready, I'm ready."

"No, it has nothing to do with me. This has to come from you. This will be the hardest work you've done yet."

"It is coming from me. If you give me permission, then I'm ready to move forward. If you believe I can do it without hurting myself, then I'm ready to try."

"Are you afraid of hurting yourself?" he asked.

"I'm afraid of setting back my healing," she said. "I don't like pain, I'm all too familiar with it. But I can deal with that."

"I think you're fully healed. What comes next is strengthening beyond what's normal. Strength that you need for flying."

Her mouth dropped open.

"But Dr. Cosby told me, it would be three years before I could fly."

"And it might be. No one can tell. She does tend towards the worst case scenario. Did you know her daughter was a flyer?"

"No," said Caer.

"Evelyn Cosby?" asked Gregor, looking intently into her eyes.

Caer's whole body shuddered and she covered her mouth with her hand.

Evelyn Cosby had been a dancer with the London Aerial Ballet. One of their best. Caer had learned to dance watching videos of her over and over and over.

Evelyn had been dancing Swan Lake, when something went oh so wrong. The media never uncovered who was responsible, if anyone. Too many dancers onstage at once, scenery that wasn't anchored well enough. Evelyn had gotten tangled up in wires from the falling scenery and took out three other dancers. Two died, another never flew again. Evelyn had many operations to try to fix her nearly severed wing. After five years of trying to heal, she dove off the tallest building in London. And never tried to open her wings.

Caer had been ten at the time. Completely horrified that her idol had died. Even more horrified that she'd given up.

"So you see why Dr. Cosby isn't very optimistic about someone's chances of recovery. She still hasn't gotten over her own daughter's death."

Caer nodded and stood up straighter.

"I'm not Evelyn Cosby. She couldn't heal because she killed two dancers and ruined the life of another. It wasn't true, but that's probably how she saw it. I will heal. And fly again. And I will dance again."

"Okay," he said, tossing the orange peel into the trash and returning to his place in the middle of the room. "So the Company is paying me a preposterous amount of money to help you. Let's get on with it. From now on, everything we do is focused on strengthening you. Preparing you to fly again, without losing what conditioning you have left. We need forward movement!"

He clapped his hands and motioned for her to start doing wing exercises. She began with the basic movements that beginning flyers started with. Holding each of the five positions until her right wing trembled. Then she released it, folding it up, but holding her left wing until it too trembled.

Her heart beamed, full of hope. She hadn't realized how much despair had ruled her life since the accident. She'd been all bravado. But it had been empty. Just a facade.

This felt real. He'd given her hope back again. She could do this.

She'd fly again.

CHAPTER 27 - ANGUS

ANGUS SAT IN THE GLASSED IN ROOM, WAITING FOR RODRIGUEZ. This time he was on the free side of the glass, not as a prisoner. It felt better.

Rodriguez had agreed to meet without his lawyer. Not very smart, but Angus didn't really care about Rodriguez' relationship to Jonas. He just wanted the truth about the cells.

A door opened on the other side of the glass and a guard ushered Jonathon into the room. He looked sallow. He certainly looked depressed. Hadn't bothered to brush his shaggy hair. He sat in the chair, not meeting Angus' eyes.

"Hello Jonathon."

Jonathon grunted.

Then finally asked, "What do you want?"

"I want to know what you put in the growth cells."

Jonathon looked up, his eyebrows raised in surprise.

"Why?"

"Because it's what changed the building. I want to know what happened."

"Do you own the company again?"

"It's too soon to tell. But even if I don't get it back, I want to know what caused such a strange reaction."

"Jonas told me to screw up the building. He didn't specify. I added some dust from a pulverized meteorite."

Angus whistled and leaned back in his chair. "And that's all? That's what caused all the strange growth?"

Jonathon nodded. "There might still be some of it left in a brown paper bag in my locker outside the building. He told me to get rid of it. I couldn't. Not after seeing what amazing things the building could do."

"Wow. Did you know what the meteorite was made of?"

"No, at first I just meant to contaminate the cells. Then after it grew out of control, I didn't have time to analyze the dust. I meant to," Jonathon said, hanging his head.

"Well, if I get the company, I'll try to find out. Provided your locker's still there."

"How is the building?"

"Still growing, as far as I can tell at a distance. They look beautiful, the first one revived the second, you know."

"I'd heard."

"And they're both growing together, beautifully. What's inside, I have no idea, but I'd love to see."

"You didn't want to kill the building did you? Jonas told me you did."

"Not after it became apparent that it was sentient. How could I? All those orders came from the Board. If I get the Core Growth back, I'll be choosing my own Board."

"Good. I hope it works out. I'm sorry I tried to shoot you. That was one of my more irrational choices."

"Yeah, it was. Sorry things turned out this way. But pleading guilty will get you off sooner."

"That's why I did it. I mean I did pull the trigger. No denying that."

"Was my father involved?"

"Jonas said he was. I never talked to him."

"No, he'd keep his hands clean. String Jonas out to hang, though."

Jonathon nodded.

"Anything else you want to tell me about the cells?"

"No. If you can't find my locker, I bought the meteorite chunk at a rock and gem show. That won't help you much. I can't remember the vendor's name."

"Okay, I'll see if I can find your locker," said Angus. He got up to leave and said, "Take care of yourself. I'll put in a good word for you."

Jonathon nodded.

Angus walked out of the room and left the building. He breathed in the fresh air. Pollen filled, but fresh. Not recycled.

He called his car and got inside. He sent a message to Otis. "See if you can get the contents of Jonathon Rodriguez locker at the building site. Especially looking for a brown paper bag filled with rocks or dust. It's very precious."

Then he messaged Willa, "Finished talking to Jonathon. Keep him safe if you can."

He had the car drive over the bridge to Capital Island and to an overlook and got out. In the drizzle, he watched the two buildings twining together. They looked like lovers cuddling together as dusk drew near.

Like he wanted to be with Caer.

He should go to the Company's Complex. He should talk to her. She knew he was getting out today. He'd told her yesterday afternoon.

And hadn't had a chance to see her yet.

Inside the car, his screen flickered on and he saw Willa at a news conference.

"Yes, at this time, the Zephyr Ballet Company of New Seattle will be filing charges against Mr. Gregory Speares and Mr. Jonas Speares for substantial damages. We are a family and we spend years developing our dancers. That involves considerable training. The housing, insurance and other costs would make your head spin. Mr. Gregory Speares insisted the performance take place in their building, not ours. We have security at ours. He assured us that our dancers would be safe. Instead one of our principal dancers has lost the ability to fly, perhaps forever. She very nearly lost her life. This is horrifying. She's had twelve grueling operations to repair her wing. It will be years before we know if she can fly again. And even longer before she could possibly dance again. We hold both Gregory Speares and Jonas Speares fully responsible. I will not go into further details of their involvement, tonight."

The media continued to question her about Caer and her recovery. Willa downplayed any hint that Caer might be recovering more quickly than Dr. Cosby predicted.

Angus waved at the parking attendant at the Complex. He was admitted inside and the car let him out near the elevator. Angus got out and the car parked itself.

He first went to the PR office. Karyn was there. She jumped out of her chair, ran around the desk and hugged him.

"I'm so glad you're out! We missed you."

"Missed my bright shiny ideas, you mean," he teased.

"Those too."

"I just wanted to warn you, Willa's announced that the Company's suing my father and Jonas. She only said it was about lack of security at the performance, so far."

Karyn nodded. "Not the best PR in the world, but I'll use it. Thanks for the heads up."

"If they fold, she'll announce the lawsuit's been withdrawn."

"Where does that leave the Company?"

"Rich, either way. I'll be the one paying. I'll be selling off all of Jonas' assets. You'll be getting the money."

"You'd do that for the Company?"

"You saved my life when I had nowhere to turn. I don't forget my friends. Also Caer's operations and physical therapy must be costing a small fortune. Jonas should pay for that. If I get Core Growth back, that's all I need. You'll do good things with the money."

Karyn nodded.

"I need to go see Caer. Any idea where she might be?"

"It's eight. Lying down somewhere with either ice or heat on her wing, I'd think," said Karyn.

He cocked his head.

Karyn said, "She's got a grueling schedule. I've never seen a dancer work as hard as she does. And that was before the injury. She and Gregor get along well. He's a workaholic."

"I'll check her apartment."

He ran up two flights, but was soon out of breath. He'd done nothing but sit in a cell lately.

He knocked on her door and heard her yell, "Open."

She sat in a chair that had blue packs of fake ice tied to it, just in the place where it cradled her right wing.

"Hi," she said, brightly. "You're out!"

"Yes, I'm out."

He sat next to her chair, on a matching dancer's chair with the narrow back. Her apartment looked messy. Clothes tossed everywhere, dishes piled next to the sink. Clutter on her table. She must be working hard.

She looked tired, despite the attempt at cheerfulness. Lines crossed her forehead and perched between her brows.

Had those lines been there when he'd first seen her? But then her face had been caked with heavy makeup, how could he have noticed them?

"How are you?" he asked.

"I'm good. Gregor's making me work really hard, but it's good. He's given me hope. He thinks I'll fly again. And much sooner than three years from now. That makes me happy. And you're free. That makes me happy too."

"I'm so pleased. I knew you'd be able to fly again. You're so strong."

He took her hand and she smiled at him.

"I don't know how you feel about me," he said. "But I love you. I have for a very long time."

"I thought you might," she said. "I love you, too."

She got up from her chair and sat on his lap. He put his arms around her. Her iced muscles felt cold to his touch.

"I don't know what the future's going to hold for me. It might get really ugly. The next 24 hours is key. I may go to war against my family, a war in the media. It'll be very public. Either that or they'll give in and I'll get my company back and all of Jonas' assets as well. Which I'll need to spend some time disposing of. The next few weeks are going to be extraordinarily busy."

"Whatever happens, I'll be here. I've got a lot of work to do. Better that you're not around to hear me whining about it."

"I've never heard you whine."

"Yes, you have. My sparkling personality just overwhelmed the whining. You didn't notice."

"It's true, you do sparkle."

She kissed him with a kiss that promised a lifetime of pleasure.

When he could breathe again, she said, "Come to bed with me. I've waited a long time for you."

And he did.

CHAPTER 28 - CAER

CAER WATCHED ANGUS PACE BEFORE HER SCREENS, WITH ONLY A towel around his waist. She fixed a pot of tea, the old fashioned way, while sweeping across the kitchen area in a long, flowing robe. She really wanted to drag him back to bed. Last night had been amazing.

But he needed to get his life cleared up first.

And she had workouts to do.

The newscasts were talking about everything except what he was interested in, apparently. He'd called Willa, the lawyer. She had no news for him, either. So he paced.

The kettle boiled on her little stove and she poured the hot water into a teapot, filled with the finest black tea from India. Then put a little crocheted cover on the pot.

She pulled two antique cups from a cupboard and set them on her now cleared off table, covered with an antique embroidered tablecloth. And the tea strainer. She pulled out a creamer, with a completely different pattern on it and filled it with cream from her tiny refrigerator.

Finally, she poured two cups of tea.

"Cream?" she asked.

"What?" he asked her, turning from the screens, looking confused.

"Do you want cream in your tea?"

"Uh, sure," he said, turning back to the screens and flipping the volume between them.

She poured cream into the two cups and went to stand behind him, wrapping her arms around him and hugging him. She loved the warm, earthy smell of his skin. She could drink it in all day.

"Come and have some tea."

His phone buzzed and he jumped and answered it.

"Hello."

"Oh, hello Otis. You got it. Wonderful. I'll pick it up later today and take it to be analyzed. Thanks."

He ran his hand through his short hair, obviously listening.

"No, no word yet, I'm on edge about it."

He paused, listening again.

"Okay, thanks. Goodbye."

Angus clicked the phone off and flicked off the screens, then came to sit at the table with the old cotton tablecloth her grandmother had embroidered. Grandma had been on a old-style crafts kick at the time she made it.

Caer gazed at him as he sipped his tea. It was hard getting used to him with blue eyes again. His eyes had been purple ever since the accident. The dye had finally gone away while he was in jail.

"What are you doing today?" he asked.

She leaned back and stretched her arms up. "What I do every day. Work out, stretch, do my physical therapy and work out some more."

He shook his head. "My god, your workouts would kill me."

She laughed. Her pre-accident work out had wiped out a local baseball player who'd wanted to try it. And it hadn't included the flying part, just her ground exercises.

"I am an athlete," she said, sipping the hot tea. The sharp flavor of the tea rolled around her mouth with the rich cream taste. She loved her tea.

His phone jingled and he answered it.

"Hello," he said.

"That's great, Willa. Okay, I'll be in this afternoon."

She watched his shoulders drop. He really had been on edge about everything. She marveled at how little she knew this man, even though she knew him intimately.

He clicked the phone off.

"We won. I got everything I asked for," he said, grinning. "I need to go sign papers this afternoon. This is the twenty-second Century and we still sign papers, but wow, I'm so excited I'm just babbling. Sorry."

"No, don't be sorry. You should be excited. Your life has been hell. Now it's turning around. I think you need your work."

"I do. I need to be doing something useful."

"You were useful to the Company."

"And I plan to continue to be useful there. I'll still work with PR. I have more ideas for them. And I hope to be very, very useful in your healing and physical therapy," he said, leaning over and nuzzling her neck, nipping at her earlobe. "I think we should finish our tea and go back to bed."

"The tea will wait," she said, getting up from the table.

His eyes widened.

She ran for the bedroom, laughing.

He followed her and flung his towel across the room.

"It's a good thing you got your company back. Business clearly excites you."

He laughed and said, "No, you excite me."

"Clearly you're going nowhere ever again," she said.

CHAPTER 29 - ANGUS

ANGUS SIGNED THE PAPERS AT WILLA'S OFFICE, IN FRONT OF TWO other lawyers. His father had already signed them. He momentarily wondered if he'd missed something. Had his father found a loophole. No, that was just second guessing. Willa had checked the papers too.

He still needed to be careful. He wouldn't put it past his father or Jonas to leave land mines lying around for him to find.

Jonas would still be in hiding. The police had refused to drop the lawsuit. Which comforted him. He hoped Jonas would be caught and convicted. For trying to kill him and nearly destroying Caer.

He took his copy of the papers and drove down to the buildings. There were a couple of engineers there, monitoring the buildings' growth, but all work on the buildings had stopped, even before the accident.

"Mr. Speares, You're back," said George.

"Yes, I own the company again."

"What's going to happen to the buildings?" asked Sam.

"I'm not sure yet. I'd like to see what they have in mind."

"You're not going to kill them?" asked George, pushing his safety helmet back on his head.

"That's not my intention. And I don't have a Board anymore to tell me that I have to."

"Good," said Sam. "Because it would be wrong."

"Why?" asked Angus.

"I can't really say how, but they're as alive as any animal is. I don't want to be non-scientific, but it understands us. It responds to our talking to it."

"How?"

"Well, the other day I remarked about blue being my favorite color, my daughter had asked me and she made me a blue scarf you see. The building turned blue and stayed that way all that day," said Sam.

"Interesting. Can you gentlemen give me a tour of the buildings? I haven't been here in what seems like forever."

"I'd love to," said Sam.

"I'll need to stay out here," said George. "Safety precautions. And Sir, you'll need to wear a hard hat."

"Of course," said Angus.

He picked up a helmet from the bin and put it on. Then followed Sam into the building.

As Angus entered, he felt as if the very building was breathing. How alive was it?

The smell was of clean, damp earth, although the entryway looked clean and dry. Very clean, as if someone had swept and mopped it. He noticed that where he and Sam and tracked in wet footprints, the water and mud had been immediately absorbed.

"If the buildings are alive, then what nourishes them?" asked Angus.

"They get their water from the air, rain and humidity, I'd guess. But nutrients? I'm not a biologist, or a buildingologist. What do plants eat?"

"Minerals, right?"

"Yeah. So far as we can tell, the buildings eat dust, dirt, debris. We tried a little experiment. There are places at the base of the buildings where dirt piles up. We found there are, like roots growing there. They take the dirt in, extract what they want and spit it back out. The soil was mounding up there. So we took some away and added fresh soil that had had different mineral components measured. Then measured it again a week later, after it was all mounded up again. It's eating the minerals."

"Where did you measure the soil at?" asked Angus.

"There's a teacher and a group of kids at the University who are fascinated by the building. He tried to work with your brother, but Mr. Speares wasn't having it. Didn't want anyone around the buildings. So we sort of let them work under the radar."

"I'll be happy to let them study things here. Would you put me in contact with them?"

"Jimmy, that's the prof, will be happy to hear that. We also tried giving the buildings contaminated soil and what do you think happened?"

"No idea."

"The buildings cleaned it all up. Ate all the contaminants. And used them up somehow. They can't be measured anywhere in the building. Jimmy had the kids measure air contaminants in the air around the city. The air surrounding the buildings out to about two miles around it, is considerably cleaner of pollutants. And you know, I feel cleaner after I leave the buildings than when I went in."

"Amazing," said Angus, his head spinning with ideas.

"Jimmy will be bugging you to get the components of the growth cells."

"I wish I knew exactly what Rodriguez did."

"Hope you can figure it out, because what a great thing for the world this could be. Too bad these buildings weren't around in the 2080's with all that deadly Asian Air. They could've cleaned it up, just like that," said Sam. He snapped his finger.

They continued walking through the empty buildings, following the walkway that entered into the other building. It felt as if the buildings pulsed. It wasn't unpleasant, actually, he felt relaxed. As if the building was comforting him, de-stressing him.

There were now several walkways between the buildings. One on every floor.

Angus touched the wall. It felt warm to his hand.

"It's soft," said Sam. "And the temperature changes in opposition to outside. It's cool in here when it's hot outside and vice versa. It feels like the buildings anticipate our needs."

"Is it still re-working the electrical, plumbing and air circulation?"

"Nope, it seems all done. In both buildings. And we hadn't even started any of that in the new building. But it's all there and in place, different than how we would have done it though. But functional. Jimmy brought in some lamps and the power system connected to them right away. Turned them on. Completely wireless. Not like my old house."

"So what you're saying is that both buildings are ready to be occupied?"

"Yeah. I think they are. Well, aside from all the inspections that need to happen. I don't see how they'll pass. The inspectors are not going to understand the plumbing or electrical system. Hell, I've been studying it and I don't even understand it."

"Well, I'd like to bring Jimmy in and hear his thoughts on all this. Before we even attempt inspections. And I'd like to have a meeting of all the engineers. I want to hear what everybody's thinking. It'll be months before we can get inspections scheduled anyway. If what these buildings do is clean things, think what that could mean for a hospital. Or for all those people with Immune Compromised Diseases. They could live here. Or if we can replicate the process, what that could mean for clean air for our world again? So many people could live fuller lives. A lot of ifs to work through."

"I like where your thinking is going, Sir."

They left the buildings and Angus was struck by how much cleaner the air was inside. And Sam was right, he actually felt cleaner after having been in the buildings.

He had his life back again. Except it was better.

His new life would be about helping to put the world back together again. And he had Caer. His heart filled with hope whenever he thought of her and how hard she worked even when she didn't believe in herself.

Now that she believed, in herself, in him, in them, there would be no stopping her. And her belief was contagious.

Together they could make the world better.

~

If you've gotten this far, would you please consider leaving an honest review? Many readers depend on reviews to help them find their next read. It doesn't take much, just a few words on your opinion of the book. It would mean so much to me. Thank you!

ABOUT THE AUTHOR

Linda Jordan writes fascinating characters, visionary worlds, and imaginative fiction. She creates both long and short fiction, serious and silly. She believes in the power of healing and transformation, and many of her stories follow those themes.

In a previous lifetime, Linda coordinated the Clarion West Writers' Workshop as well as the Reading Series. She spent four years as Chair of the Board of Directors during Clarion West's formative period. She's also worked as a travel agent, a baker, and a pond plant/fish sales person, you know, the sort of things one does as a writer.

Currently, she's the Programming Director for the Writers Cooperative of the Pacific Northwest.

Linda now lives in the rainy wilds of Washington state with her husband, daughter, four cats, a cluster of Koi and an infinite number of slugs and snails.

Her other work includes:

~*Titanian Fury*

~*Notes on the Moon People*

~*The Bones of the Earth Series: Faerie Unraveled, Faerie Contact, Faerie Descent, Faerie Flight and Faerie Confluence*

~*Living in the Lower Chakras*

~*Horticultural Homicide*

~*Continental Divide*

All her work can be found at your favorite online bookseller.

Get a FREE ebook!
Sign up for Linda's Serendipitous Newsletter at her website:
www.LindaJordan.net
She can be found on Facebook at:
www.facebook.com/LindaJordanWriter
Metamorphosis Press website is at:
www.MetamorphosisPress.com
Goodreads: https://www.goodreads.com/author/show/
2021274.Linda_Jordan

Writers love reviews, even short, simple ones and honest reviews help other readers find the book. Please go to where you bought this book, or Goodreads, and leave a review. It would be much appreciated.

www.ingramcontent.com/pod-product-compliance
Lightning Source LLC
Chambersburg PA
CBHW020614120726
47905CB00003B/786